WOLF BELLS

WOLF BELLS

A NOVEL

LENI ZUMAS

ALGONQUIN BOOKS OF CHAPEL HILL
LITTLE, BROWN AND COMPANY

Copyright © 2025 by Leni Zumas

Algonquin Books of Chapel Hill / Little, Brown and Company
Hachette Book Group
1290 Avenue of the Americas, New York, NY 10104
algonquinbooks.com

First Edition: September 2025

Algonquin Books of Chapel Hill is an imprint of Little, Brown and Company, a division of Hachette Book Group, Inc. The Algonquin Books name and logo are trademarks of Hachette Book Group, Inc.

ISBN 978-1-64375-657-8 (hardcover)
ISBN 978-1-64375-660-8 (e-book)
LCCN 2025933704

Printing 1, 2025
LSC-C
Printed in the United States of America

To everyone this world wasn't built for

A bell is a cup . . . until it is struck.

HERE AT THE BRINK OF A FOREST on a cliff above a river in a valley between haunches of limestone was a steep brown ship of a
house. The roots of the trees circling the ship had met corpses,
been shredded by hooves, and seen a freak summer when every
live thing froze. On the concrete foundation that sat on the dirt
that sat on a crust of basalt were twenty rooms, nine bathrooms,
and one porch. Metal and plastic and clay, glass and acrylic
and wood, two kinds of cedar, three kinds of fir, a hundred
deep winters stood through. Here were the dead and the living
together—things that had happened and were happening, hair
and skin from gone bodies dusting bodies in motion. Rooms of
leaky bodies with their wishes and toenails and teeth and regrets,
their tampons and catheters, nipples hard and soft, a two-haired
mole on a cheek. Static jumping in the dress of a doll on a shelf.

In 1919 a sea captain had brought his wife hundreds of
miles from the damp coast to this valley, hoping the mountain
air would cure her. In less than a month she was dead. Infected
corpses weren't allowed on trains, and no cemetery would agree
to take hers, so he bought land on the bluff above town and buried the body himself. Then he paid other men to build a house
near the grave. Thick lengths of old-growth fir, an aquarium with
mechanical air pumps. Extravagance unheard of, then, in these
mountains. The cook and housekeeper hired from town brought
back reports of their boss's profligacy: the purchase for each child
of a personal horse, or his insistence that the table linen be washed
and ironed after only one week of use. The housekeeper said the

captain sprayed his scrotum with cologne, for what reason she'd die before trying to guess.

Minerals from the grave of the captain's wife had turned into honeysuckle, been plucked, lived in water on the table, floated up their noses. Here they lived, backed up against a forest on the fringe of a dingy town, alone and together in these rooms.

Here are the rooms, and what there was room for.

Soundproofed Room

THE HALL AT THE TOP of the House was where the captain's youngest child had kept her companions, their bisque heads and cloth bodies slumped against black-rose wallpaper in order of favor: worst-loved near the window, best-loved near the banister. The captain's great-granddaughter now stood waiting to escort a soon-to-be-ex-resident downstairs. He had broken the rules too often, refused to do the few things required of him. She hated being in charge of the situation, but the House was hers, legally at least, so she stood firmly in the chilly hall while he slammed and kicked and muttered. She'd given him plenty of chances to succeed at his duties—to join the other residents for dinner, play chess or watch TV with them, and every Tuesday bring the trash and recycling bins down to the road—but he was only interested in recording songs in the room he had soundproofed with thick gray panels of egg-crate foam and a wool blanket and what looked like military-grade canvas stapled to the floor.

"This is such bullshit," he said, shoving plastic baggies of beef jerky and dried mango into a backpack. "I *did* make an effort. Those people aren't easy. The asshole with the huge forehead accused me of poisoning the night snack, did you know that? And he made implicit threats. I literally did not feel safe."

He had been at the House for six weeks. Caz referred to him as Neck Beard unless he was standing right there, in which case she called him buddy. He was an anti-cement activist who, when he wasn't chaining himself to construction equipment, worked remotely for a consumer-research firm. He'd conducted his work calls in the library, within earshot of all. Whenever someone answered but refused to do the survey, he would pretend to be calling about their tax returns and say, "We have found troubling irregularities." After hanging up, he would sometimes whisper: "Take that, America."

"I had high hopes for this place," he told Caz. "Like, the concept is really cool. Whereas the *reality*—"

"You mean the concept that you could live here for free if you participated in the community? A concept you seemed unable to grasp?"

"Oh, I grasped it. I grasped the fuck out of that little concept." He picked up a stray piece of paper, stared at it, crumpled it, and threw it into a corner. "But whatever. This is turning out for the best, because I don't actually want to live in an unheated nursing home."

"Intergenerational community," she said.

"Dude, this is a nursing home," he said. "With, like, add-ons."

Caz smiled. She didn't need to justify the House to him. He didn't take her seriously, anyway; she saw the disdain in his watery eyes. Saw him not see her, not be curious in the slightest about who she was or who she had been.

The rag rug under her feet stank of piss. Walking the dog was another House chore currently being neglected, though not by Neck Beard. The hallway on this floor had smelled bad even before Fronzi started peeing on it. Industrial-solvent bad, as though the wallpaper glue were releasing noxious fumes, which it probably was.

"Key?" she said.

"Huh?"

"I'll need your house key."

He scratched the dark-blond fuzz on his jaw. "No idea where

that is, to be honest. But don't worry, I'm not planning to come back in the dead of night and steal your TV that was manufactured before my birth."

"Mail it to me when you find it," she said.

"Best of luck with your concept," he said.

"Dick," she whispered. He was a sweaty white boy in a cowrie-shell necklace who thought he knew more about music than she did and whose zeal for battling environmental destruction was obviously performative.

At the end of the hall was a small window tilted diagonally under the eave, a witch window, its crooked angle meant to prevent witches from steering their broomsticks into the house. Through the pane came a slippery light that fell on both of them as they lugged his bags to the stairs, the weak sun seeping through clouds massed above the valley to hit the House and the trees and the river below.

Office

CAZ PULLED APART HER BRAIDS and raked her fingers through the bleach-crisped strands, then cleaned her glasses with the hem of her shirt, thinking she really should spend the crumb of energy it would take to find the cloth the optometrist had given her but fuck the cloth, she would eat black licorice instead. From the bag in the drawer she pulled out several sticky tubes and laid them in a row on the desk.

She should go check on Mr. Rudd. His urine had been leaking onto his clothes, and because he wore the same pants for days without showering, he kept getting UTIs. They'd had to do a second round of antibiotics for the last infection. He complained about smelling piss but wouldn't accept that it was his own piss. Lasko and Davey took turns helping him take showers, and Caz tried to make sure he was changing his clothes regularly.

She would go in a minute.

Evidently (she'd seen a headline) you could die from eating too much black licorice. She ate it with abandon and had reached the age of sixty-three in decent health, even if some days, like today, her body felt lumped and brittling, as though in the inner pipe of each bone some crucial fluid was drying up. Drying things scared her. She used to have a recurring nightmare in which the upper half of her face, for medical reasons, had been torn away, leaving her eyes bobbing on stalks. She scream-begged the doctors to reattach the skin but the skin had withered to paper before they could sew it back on.

Stretching, it occurred to her, might counteract the drying. Restore her wetness. With licorice sticking out of her mouth, she got on the floor and lay on her back and pulled one knee to her chest, then the other. Something hit the window (a pebble? a nut?), and Caz's first thought was that it had been thrown for her. To get her attention. She laughed at her own grandiosity, a regular laugh, not the Dracula giggle. At a show in Los Angeles once, some white-power bikers had shot a guy in the parking lot while she and the band were onstage, and the club had shut off the power, and out of nervousness, to fill the dark, Caz kept doing the Dracula giggle into a useless microphone: "A-wah-ha-ha, a-hoo-hoo-ha-*ha*, my pretty!" Pathetic, as Vara was happy to remind her later on.

A tree had thrown the nut. Not Davey.

"There you are," Vara said now from the office doorway.

"Here I am." Caz pointed her toes toward the ceiling.

Rolling into the room: "Will you help me do my cream?"

"Yeah. I also need to ask you . . ." Point, flex. Point flex. "If you're ready for me to post the ad?"

Vara's face did not move. "Go ahead."

"You sure? Because last time we talked about—"

"I was having a bad day, and I overreacted."

"You can't keep doing it all yourself."

"I am aware." Vara held out the cold tube of cream. "But how do you plan to pay this person? Sell the back acre?"

Caz jumped up from the floor. "Already sold it."

"Seriously?"

"In March. For taxes. God, don't look so *withering!*" Caz squirted a worm of medication along the inside of Vara's wrist. "We can fill Neck Beard's bedroom with a paying resident, once we get rid of the soundproofing. Wait, is that my sweater?"

Vara looked down at a pink-and-charcoal-striped wool sleeve. "You gave it to me. Three years ago."

"Did I?"—gently rubbing cream across the thick blue veins.

"Don't worry," Vara said, "you'll get it back when I die."

"Drama!"

"I'm just saying facts. Am I allowed to say facts?"

"And we need to reassign Beardy's chores to the others."

"You must be absolutely shattered to see him go."

"Well, he wasn't a great fit. Kestrel's been on dog walking and the Fish Bowl vacuuming, and Davey's been on laundry, and Ant is—what, mopping the infirmary? Let's keep them on that but take Davey off laundry and give him trash and dog, and switch Kestrel to laundry."

"Please don't put Fronzi's life in the hands of that gun-wielding person."

"He doesn't *wield* a gun," Caz said. "He just owns one."

"Isn't that bad enough? Give Fronzi to Ant."

"They're too busy with their dissertation."

"What about House expectations? The failure to abide by which just led you to kick someone out?"

"We could ask Marika—I think she likes the dog."

"She likes nothing," Vara said. "She is a liker of zero things."

"I don't love you," Caz sang, "for your graveyard eyes."

"I don't love you," Vara mumbled, "for your shaven thighs."

Caz capped the tube and wiped her hands on her jeans. "So I can go ahead and post the ad?"

"Don't you need to be getting to school?"

"I only teach on Mondays and Wednesdays."

"Today is Wednesday."

"Fuck, really?" Caz opened her laptop. "No, thank God, it's Thursday. Happy Halloween, by the way."

Vara stared at her hands, which glistened from the medication, and Caz knew she was thinking of what Halloween used to mean but no longer did. Vara had been a melancholy person the day they met, fifty-one years ago, and had shown no interest in changing since.

Fish Bowl

CYPRESS BRANCHES SCRAPED against the oriel window of the room most essential to the life of the House. A gash in the floorboard—the sea captain had once thrown a hammer out of boredom and grief—caught the wheels of Vara's chair, the rubber nub of Mr. Rudd's walker. The smell of hot garlic seeped in from the kitchen, the iron radiators hissed, and a romantic sitcom set in London had begun. Today's episode was about the husband character trying to write a memoir and it was *hard* and the wife character had to console him while they drank French-press coffee, their posh accents bouncing through the garlicky air.

On the green couch, Kestrel nestled deep in the velour cushions. She found this show unwatchably dull but liked being among them, the olds in their quilted vests and compression socks, one of them knitting with yarn that smelled like smoke. When they laughed at a punchline, she laughed, too, just to feel the roof of her mouth vibrate with theirs.

On the plaid couch, their knees almost but not quite touching, Davey and Caz played cards.

"It's true!" she said, running her tongue along the nine of hearts.

"Aw, what? No."

"Most men are very, very bad at it. *Very* bad."

"I beg thee to differ." He snuffled up a long glob of mucus, then swallowed it.

"On what basis? Slapjack."

They slapped. She was faster and grabbed the pile.

"On the basis," Davey said, "of knowledge of my own talents, which are so off the chain there's not even a chain."

"*Are* they," she said.

"In that department? Yeah. And in the department of handling an M4A1 carbine. Slapjack."

Caz took the pile again. "Gunnilingus."

She was a million years old and still looked good, which confused and thrilled Davey. What if he were to reach over right now and run his fingers through her platinum-blond hair? She'd probably like it. What if he were to ask if he could snort Wellbutrin off her bare ass? She'd probably say yes.

"No customer left satisfied." He blinked hard. "I mean, no customer is left *un*satisfied."

"Oh, so you charge for it?" She sounded slightly bored, and he wanted her more.

"I don't," he said, "but I should."

Group home seeks certified nursing assistant, 10-15 hrs/
week, for tasks including meds dispensing, bathing, wound
care, & catheters. We are a vibrant multigenerational community that welcomes all. Must have own car (we aren't
on a bus line).

Dining Room

AS SHE STOOD heaping her plate with carrots, bread, and fish in a thin brown sauce, Caz became aware of a presence behind her, quietly expectant. She waited a few beats but the presence remained. Finally Lasko said, "Have I ever told you that your music got me through high school?"

She smiled. "Shut up, really?" He had told her this several times.

"Not to fan-boy too pathetically."

"Aw."

"I think I broke my CD player on 'Freezing Summer.'"

"When I wrote that song," Caz told him, "I thought the year 'Eighteen Hundred and Froze to Death' was proof that climate problems had always been a thing, like they came and went as part of the natural cycle, so we didn't need to worry. Can you imagine being that fucking clueless?"

The song had been used later in a TV commercial for Icelandic tourism. Lasko wondered if she would also mention the irony of choosing a song about people starving during an environmental disaster to advertise a country you need an airplane to reach, but she did not.

"You know another one I adored?" he said. "'Inheritance Powder.' 'Scenic venom down your throat / and the sun / is on foot / in you.' I quoted that once in a letter to my ex. The metaphor of love being a poison we willingly swallow."

"It wasn't a metaphor." Caz sat down next to Adeline, who was cradling Tufty the owl in the crook of her arm. Davey was scraping a spoon against his front teeth. Marika had fallen asleep with her eyes half-open, chin dipping into collar-tucked napkin.

"Oh!" Blushing, Lasko plunked down his plate.

"'Inheritance powder' is a term for arsenic. I never wrote songs about love. Those were Vara's. She wrote the sappy ones."

"Do you mind if I ask, I mean, I've always kind of wondered, why you weren't called *The* Bolts?"

"Vara wanted just Bolts because it could be either a noun or a verb, and because it was a symbol of both the domestic—fabric— and the sublime—lightning."

"Cool . . ."

"We used to get reviews with headlines like 'Bolts, No Nuts.' And they'd just talk about how my ass looked, or the fact that Vee could play guitar really well, which in those days was shocking."

Lasko nodded gravely.

Almost gone, that world she'd spent a life in. Traces in songs, photographs, films, a few buildings in downtown Manhattan. Traces in strands in the seams of brains soon to crumble in their skulls. Her own strands, too. And who cared? Did the people of the future need to know the set list played by X band at Y club on Z date? Or the fact that A singer slept with B drummer's girlfriend while they were recording C record? None of it mattered unless you'd been there; and even if you had, how much could it possibly matter now? To shake off the dismalness, Caz said, "Mr. Rudd! You haven't picked the Community Question in a while."

"Quite a good reason for that," he said.

"Even if you think it's silly—"

"Silly don't begin to capture it."

"Regardless, would you do us the honor? And remember, guys, just say the first thing that occurs to you. Whatever's sitting right there at the top of your mind."

Rudd sighed. "When you were young, what did you read on the crapper?"

"*Guns and Ammo*," Davey said.

"When I was growing up?" Adeline said.

Caz, softly: "What's a book you remember reading?"

Adeline brought her napkin to her lips. "*Cherry Ames, Cruise Nurse. Cherry Ames, Flight Nurse.*"

"Just the one, Adeline."

"*Cherry Ames, Department Store Nurse.*"

"Why would a department store need a nurse?" Marika said, not asleep after all. "And I will pass."

"Same," Kestrel said.

"Then we're done."

"I didn't get to go," Mrs. Quimbee pointed out.

"Jesus God."

"May I have a turn?"

"We're ableeze with curiosity."

"My preferred toilet reading was either Jane Austen or Charles—"

"JUST THE BLOODY ONE!"

"But Adeline got to do three."

"Do people often fall ill at department stores?"

Caz peeled the crust from a bread slice and tried to sculpt the middle into a ball. Whole wheat and homemade, it wasn't pliable enough. She missed factory bread, though she would never have admitted this to Lasko.

Davey dipped his head to sniff the plate. "What the fuck kind of fish is this?"

"Orange roughy."

"That sounds like pubic hair."

"How have you never heard of orange roughy?"

"Because I'm extremely ignorant," Davey said.

"Did y'all know," Kestrel said, "that the word *trumpen* is Swedish for 'sullen and morose'?"

"How about it's IKEA for 'toilet-paper holder.'"

"I'm not kidding. Look it up."

Picking at his teeth with fork tines, Davey said, "I would, if I cared more?"

"The name of my mother," Adeline said, "means 'gem of the sea.'"

Caz took Adeline's hand. The skin was shiny and cold. There was still loneliness in a place set up to solve it.

CUSTARD, CARROTS, AND ROUGHY broke down in bellies. Marika threw today's underpants into the closet, on top of a plastic container of mozzarella sticks, got under the covers, and reached to touch the pinecone on her nightstand, her brother's pinecone, his best-loved thing. *Kalinikta, koukounári.* Vara was crying and Caz was rubbing her back. Mr. Rudd dreamed of running and kicking. Ant played a wooden-block game on their phone. Kestrel texted her best friend: "happy birthday, my ghoul! How does it feel to be twatty-nine?" while uploading a hundred words on sarcophagi to the web encyclopedia she freelanced for. Davey masturbated to a hot grocery-store cashier being yelled at by her supervisor, then to Caz soaping her tits, then back to the cashier and the supervisor fucking in a closet. Three swifts arranged their wings on the chimney crown. Two boxelder bugs and a death-watch beetle crouched in the wall. Fronzi, on a pile of kitchen towels, dreamed of her mother. Over the House and all its souls, the skies ran black and fast and cold.

Kitchen

ON THE WALK downstairs at six a.m., the quiet was soft against Caz's skin. The one holiday she still liked was over. No more apples to stud with cloves (something she had never done but annually thought about doing) or pumpkin lights to string up around the front door. Now there was only November.

Washing chapped hands she thought *lotion?* then forgot lotion because somebody had left a night-snack bowl crusting on the counter. Dreggy splotches to scrub. Rinse, you fuckers, rinse! She maneuvered the biggest pot under the faucet for oatmeal water. She would give them oatmeal and fruit cup and the foil-wrapped kisses because not a single trick-or-treater had turned up for them the previous evening. Adeline wouldn't remember that chocolate killed dogs and might try to feed some to Fronzi; they needed to keep an eye out. Caz didn't want to deal with how Vara would feel if anything happened to the dog, who trembled now at her feet with round brown gazing eyes and floppy ears the color of old blood.

"You're a criminal," Caz said, bending to scratch behind her ears, "but quite an extremely adorable criminal." In the pantry she unscrewed the treat jar, and Fronzi peed on a thirty-pound sack of rice. "Seriously?" Caz tossed her a biscuit and wondered if she was obligated to transfer the rice to a non-peed-on container; decided not. Urine was sterile, and rice got boiled. Cavalier King Charles spaniels were supposed to make excellent emotional-support animals, although Caz hadn't cared about breeds when she got her; she had cared about "free and already trained." What sort of trained? Not potty, it turned out. Or if potty, then subpar potty.

In addition to rice bags and the floorboards on the third floor, Fronzi liked to anoint the woven mat in the laundry room.

Between the butcher block and the refrigerator was an opening in the wall smaller than a window, bigger than a heating vent, covered by white-painted latticework. When he first started working here, Lasko had asked what it was, perhaps imagining some quaint apparatus like a cold closet, where in olden times homemade butter would be kept fresh by an ice block and sawdust and rabbit fur. Caz, shrugging, had said: "A place for the bodies?" She pawed now through frosty bundles in the freezer, each labeled in Lasko's neat block letters. His favorite breakfast was veggie sausage, and on his mornings off, she liked to cook a batch especially for him. They should've bought more on the last grocery run; Caz was annoyed until she remembered there might be some in the chest freezer out back.

Beard of fog along the river. Pale streaks in the dark sky. From here you could see the tallest peak in the range. Did snow up there taste different from snow on the valley floor? The porch's disorder grated on Caz, all the old furniture, the bags of bottles and cans, moss thick in the cracks on the rails. She needed to organize a serious cleaning soon. Enlist Lasko and Kestrel and Davey and whatever new young had by then moved into the room vacated by the anti-cement activist.

Before she could raise the freezer lid, she heard a rustling.

It had been months since the mice in the piano. An unfun period of traps, screams, and fumigation.

More rustling from the corner, where a three-legged table was stashed under a blue tarp.

Caz listened.

The tarp's hem twitched.

She went to get the broom.

Back at the tarp: no twitching.

"I know you're in there!" she shouted, raising the broom high. Could be a whole army of them. An invasion.

A soft human cough.

Broom down. "Hello?"

Another cough.

She leaned over to pinch the corner of the crackly blue polyester, and lifted.

IF THE SEA captain's wife had not caught the Spanish flu. If he had not brought her to the mountains. If the House had not been built. None of these souls colliding.

THEY HAD CLIMBED across the night, the wind pushing at her body draped by his, one body made of two, unsteady in the dark. A white bedsheet over them. Barely a moon. Her fears: what if he woke up, what if he didn't. The sheet had holes cut out for the eyes and mouth, but it was harder to breathe under it, and her lips were chapping and she had to lick them a lot and there was a briny taste on the backs of her teeth and she couldn't spit it out because her spit had dried away. Attack by animal was a lesser fear, not in the top three. The girl had never had so many fears at once, it was thrilling, she felt knife-shaped. Boy on her back, heavy bag in one hand, the other hand holding a flashlight to slap away anything coming—tree branch, wild dog, train.

Car lights blinked across the river, high up, on the road to the city. If they fell from the cliff their heads would explode on the tracks. She wouldn't let them fall but it was interesting to know that they could. Branches and branches and black-gray sky. A noise: human? Only the whimper of the boy, dreaming. The near-frozen air made the sheet feel wet even though it was dry. She wore two pairs of pants, two shirts, a lost-and-found ski sweater, and her purple windbreaker. She was still cold. She ran cold. The boy ran hot, little furnace—loved any room with air conditioning.

Branches, sky, branches, a gnarling canopy. The girl liked trees but there was no time to think about them.

They had ridden to the top of the cliff on the municipal elevator, which looked like a flying saucer on a pole bolted into the limestone. There was a ghost (herself and the boy) and a vampire and a rushed attempt at a clown. The guy who drove the elevator had said "Pretty scary!" in a bored, rude voice that made her feel relieved because it meant he wasn't paying attention. She didn't breathe on the ride from the bottom of the cliff, which took eighteen seconds. She handled being scared by remembering a time that was scarier. Her go-to was always the hair tourniquet, two years ago. The boy's little toe turned gross colors and she couldn't figure out how to loosen the lasso of strangling hair (it was too tight on the skin to cut) and the boy was first yelling then screaming. She called a taxi and paid with the emergency twenty from the rooster box and kept thinking what if his toe died from lack of blood? At the ER they wanted to know why an eleven-year-old was bringing a six-year-old to the hospital with no parents in sight, and the girl pointed out that she was almost twelve. They called the police. The police wanted to speak to her guardian. A caseworker was assigned; there was a home visit. During the home visit the girl's aunt said if this much energy were put into actually taking care of kids instead of villainizing mothers, *that* might be a society she'd want to live in, and because of her "agitated demeanor" the caseworker scheduled more visits.

From the elevator they had walked along in a swell of trick-or-treaters and drunk teenagers until the entrance to North River Park. All they had to do was get through the park, then it wouldn't be much farther. She had memorized the map.

The path narrowed and curved away from the river, into the trees, until the wind and the car lights were gone. The girl wanted to sit down but was too nervous. Her shoulders hurt and her hands hurt from holding the bag. She was switching hands every few minutes now. She reached back to touch the boy's leg, dangling from the left duct-taped hole in the backpack, warm and loose in sweatpant cotton.

There was a two-lane road. A mailbox. A banner on the side of a church:

A FAMILY FOR EVERYONE!
Sunday Worship 11 A.M.

Then the road stopped. Dirt and grass stretched to a house with a roof gable thrust like a prow, one lit window on the highest floor. The small ghost went up the long gravel driveway and around the back, stepping carefully through crunchy drifts of leaves. The boy's pee was wafting from his diaper. One shoe made a soft pressure on the porch step, and inside the kitchen the long red ear of the dog flicked up, but the dog was too sleepy and warm on her towel to investigate. The foot inside the shoe was too numb to notice the give in the step's rotting wood. Even in mountain air, things rotted: lettuce and cherries, the flesh of a tree, the lungs of a sea captain's wife.

The porch was chaotic with objects. She found space under a table half-covered with a blue tarp and squatted and pulled off the bedsheet and arranged it on the cold boards. Eased off the backpack and cradled the boy's head as she lowered him down. He was breathing. His eyes were open a little bit, even in sleep. She took off his sweatpants and removed the pee-soaked diaper, which smelled like cornflakes, and dropped it into a plastic bag. Tugged a new diaper over his legs. Pulled the sweatpants back on. Spread the hotel towel over him and piled all the clothes from the bag (three pairs of her underwear, two pairs of his pants, his dinosaur skull shirt) onto the towel.

Eyelids sore and fluttery, adrenaline clanging in her ribcage, she took bites of a shortbread cookie between sips from the water bottle. Her plan was to wait for morning then find the music teacher.

The boy was breathing and the girl was breathing and the mountains around them were humming, long swells of voltage heaving through limestone and granite, shivering into the trees. The hum throbbed in her forehead, her jaw. It would be fine. Would it be fine? The mountains reminded her: she was a knife. She could cut a new life. She planned to be a slut (because sluts healed quicker) and an architect of debris. She planned to give not one single fuck.

Back Porch

THE GIRL WAS DREAMING of a refrigerator full of cheesecakes of different colors and sizes, some with slices taken out of them, others whole. When she tried taking out the chocolate-and-strawberry one, she couldn't because it was stuck to the shelf and so cold it burned her fingers.

"Should we call 911?"

It was a crime to steal cheesecakes, but she hadn't stolen this one yet.

"No, no—I know them from the school. Nola, hey. Can you wake up now?"

The cop was pulling on her foot. Her eyes popped open and it wasn't a cop, it was the music teacher. Nola felt gorgeously relieved. Then she felt: *but they're going to be pissed.* She sat up, hitting her head on the table they were under. "I'm sorry we're, um, but—"

"It's fine," the teacher said. "You just surprised us."

A small, freckled guy standing next to the teacher said, "Is the other one okay? He seems, like, super deeply asleep."

"I'm sorry we surprised you, Ms. Pultti."

"No 'miz,' remember? It's 'Caz.'"

"I like your necklace."

"Thanks." The freckled guy touched his raven amulet. "Are you hungry?"

"Hold on, though," Caz said. "What the fuck exactly are you doing here?"

"They were hurting him," Nola said.

"Who?"

"My cousin. The caseworkers were hurting him, so we had to leave." She watched the teacher's face change. Caz knew the basics of their situation.

"Oh, hey, don't cry." The guy knelt down to pat Nola's shoulder, fixing Caz with a severe glance. "They're probably so hungry."

"Well, let's get them some food," she said. "But then—"

"Thank you so much. Thank you. I'm gonna wake up my cousin." Nola turned to the guy. "He doesn't talk, so if you ask him something, he's not being rude that he doesn't answer."

"Okay. My name's Lasko, by the way. Do you like oatmeal?"

"Yes, but he—do you have any, just, bread?"

"Of course. Wow, though." Lasko frowned. "How long have you two been out here?"

"It's not that cold," she said quickly. "And my cousin's basically a polar bear." She ran her thumb under his chin. "Little bear," she whispered, "we're here."

James clung to sleep.

She put her lips on his earlobe and said, "Come on, it's time for breakfast," and squeezed his hand hard. He wrenched it away. Then he opened his long-lashed eyes, yawned, gave a little yowl. Yawned again.

Library

MARIKA WAS CURLED in the window seat, hidden from view by drapes and a fake-leather armchair. This was one of her morning places. She liked to sit for a long time unnoticed and watch the trees. Pulses of light were opening the iron-blue sky; the swifts were talking on the chimney crown; a mozzarella stick was warm in her fist.

The door opened to voices, feet.

Vara: "Now what?"

Caz: "Let me think for a minute."

Then an unfamiliar voice, a bright squall.

And a second new voice: "Have you read all of these books?"

Caz: "God, no."

Marika nudged the drape aside to see a girl in a ski sweater and a boy with dark hair straight and heavy past his ears, every inch of him dancing, bending forward and up, forward and up, twirling something she couldn't see in his fingers.

"Where are his shoes?" Caz said.

"He doesn't like wearing shoes," the girl said. She scooted across the room to the armchair. Marika could hear her shallow, whistling breath through the upholstery between them. The bare-foot boy pounded the floor with one palm, singing, and Marika's tongue tasted the astringent gleam of artichoke. Teeth shearing the fleshy leaf. Lemon, dill, honey.

"Maybe he would like to meet Fronzi," Vara said. "Should we bring in Fronzi?"

Library

THIS FLOOR SMELLED COLDER than the hotel floor. Tiny water glowed in a window. A shaky dog smell, dog tongue gray and hot, was jumping near James. Too much jumping—it cracked the air and hurt the floor. He yelled, which hurt the front of his head, which already hurt.

The jumping stopped.

High, fast voice: "I thought he would like her."

Scraped-velvet voice: "Well, he doesn't."

James twirled his shoelace. The window water went faster. He was aching behind his eyes and he could still smell the dog's jittery gray heat, which made him want to leave, so he started to.

"Nope," Nola said. "Stay right there, bear."

He tried again, lunging toward the door.

Nola's hands clamped onto his elbows. "I know you don't want to stay. I *know*."

If she knew, why didn't she help?

He bit her wrist.

"Oh sweetie—"

"I'm fine," Nola said.

The shoelace flicked and spiraled, safe in his fingers. Faster went the water in the window, filling with light: one strand green, one black, the others nothing. He liked how they felt in his eyes until the light was spilling and flying and sickening bright.

"How old is he?" the high, fast voice said.

He needed to go somewhere darker.

"Eight," Nola said. "Okay, I know," shoving away his clutching hand. "Sorryhesjustkindofdysregulatedrightnow."

"Is he still hungry?"

Nola wasn't helping with the light. He whirled the shoelace faster.

"Hold *on*," she said. Turning away: "Do you have any saltines?"

"Enoughforathousandships."

He went behind the couch, looking for darker. Down on his knees he threw his forehead at the floor, which didn't help enough, his head still hurt, and Nola yelled "Never do that!" and he laughed at the ridged ribbon of her anger. The shoelace fell out of his hand; it couldn't be on the floor. He picked it up and looked at the door.

A mother smell, but not *his* mother, gathered him in a blue shining. His thighs unclenched and he sagged into the shining, his fingers on the thin, dry forearm of this little mother, not his.

"Yourejustalittleapplearentyou," she said in a scraped-velvet voice. He stood held by the blue, pressing his fingers into her arm, almost touching the bone through the rubbery paper of her skin. "She said you like saltines." She opened her fist, revealing a small stack. He took the whole stack, to make sure they wouldn't be gone, and put the first two in his mouth: hard salt, oh yes, he loved that salt, that hardness. Far superior to the cloudy, sagging crackers at the hotel.

Library

NOLA WANTED SECONDS of the oatmeal, which was the best she'd ever tasted: milky, spicy, sweet. When the freckled guy came back, she would ask for more. They were alone now—James, quiet for the moment, munching crackers—in the library of the school for the dying. Stained-glass windows and haunted furniture.

Caz had said she wouldn't call the police or CPS until she talked to Stell.

But she could be lying.

What was the next plan, if Caz was lying? Like going up a tree: when one branch broke, you jumped to another. Nola had a sleeve-and-a-half of shortbread cookies and seventeen dollars. Four bus rides each. With the free transfers they could spend, theoretically, four days riding from one part of the city to another. Non-theoretically, they wouldn't last two hours.

The saltines were done. Soon he'd be noisy again. When it was just her and James, she didn't care; in the presence of another person, she couldn't *not* care. She wasn't able to stand by and watch them be bothered—she felt she must apologize, distract. She took him out of rooms when he got too screechy; she smiled and led him away before the woman in the checkout line could look disturbed. At the school for the dying, where could she take him? No one else was in the library, but screeches carried, and old people got annoyed fast. One time when they were picking up pizza James had shouted near the ear of a man with a hearing aid and the man had jumped out of his chair, flapping in agony ("God*dammit!*") and Nola yanked James out the door, too embarrassed to wait for their order.

In the placement they'd had before the hotel, everyone watched TV, all the time, constantly. Which had been fine with Nola. It was a relaxing way to be with other people. You didn't have to talk, but you *could*, at commercials. James didn't like sitting still; the most he would watch was the length of a video for a favorite song—"A Hole at the Bottom of the Sea," "The Skeleton Dance," or "10 Monsters in the Bed." He mostly roamed, or tried to get Nola to get up and go with him to the kitchen. Whether he was hungry or not, it was kitchens he liked best of any room: opening the fridge, banging the doors of the cabinets he could reach, climbing up on the counter with his shoelace.

He started pulling on her now, little claws in the softest part of her arm, making the sound that meant *come with me right this second*. She needed to cut his nails.

"We're just staying here for a minute," she said, "just in this room, okay?"

Possibly the teacher was calling CPS now. Or the cops.

Nola looked around for what they could take if they needed to leave fast, anything that could be eaten or slept on or sold. But it was pretty much just the books, the furniture, and a creepy doll on a shelf looking down on the room with shark eyes. The doll might have been an antique. Nola reached up for it, smelling dust and oldness; James pinched her ankle; she kicked him away and fingered the stiff fabric of the pink dress. Would the doll come alive and kill them for intruding upon the library? Nola would destroy the doll before it could touch her cousin. She would slam it against a wall until its head popped off. Which James would think was really funny. The doll looked old but not antique-old, not worth money, and her face, Nola saw now, was badly scratched.

Don't lose him, Nola, you can't lose him.

I promise!

Promise again.

I promise double.

She could fake a meltdown if she had to. And she had had to before. She had pretended to be "crazy," a word that meant so many things it meant pretty much nothing at all. You could call anyone crazy who you didn't like or were scared of.

Her stomach hurt a little, or maybe her uterus. That general region.

She should get James into a fresh diaper. "Come on, bear," she said, "let's go change you." There must be a ton of bathrooms in this house. And for later, for tonight, there had to be an attic room or a servant's quarter, some unused corner—there had to be—where she and the boy could fit.

Downstairs Bathroom

BLOOD COULD LEAVE a bathroom by the toilet, sink, or shower drain. Blood could leave a bathroom by the mopped-up floor. Most blood left with water, which if you didn't pay your bill could be shut off, and to get it turned back on you needed to pay the disconnect fee plus a new deposit plus whatever you had owed before. How much blood had come through this bathroom with its bony radiator and no fan and two sets of black-painted drawers built into the wall, a room old enough to have seen its share of blood, from people now dead? Flushed away, wiped away, scrubbed with hard white soap away?

The bottom half of each wall was pink tile and the top half was paper, a field of green and gold waves. James kept reaching for the flush handle and Nola kept blocking him with her forearm. She'd already taken the toilet-paper roll out of its holder and stowed it in one of the drawers so he wouldn't mess with it. She would need to find all the other bathrooms and hide their toilet paper, too. The green, gold, pink, and black looked good together, she thought. James snuck past her arm and got a rogue flush in; he watched from the corner of his eye for her reaction.

"I'm not mad," she said. These people could afford a few extra flushes. Nobody was going to shut off their water.

She looked at her underwear again: bloodless. It might not even have been her period, this harsh, folded feeling above her pubic bone; maybe it was just tiredness, or stomach flu? God, she would've loved to get sick right now—like *really* sick, out of commission, can't-move, needs-to-sleep-forever sick.

There were six diapers left, which should get them to tomorrow morning, unless James had one of his epic nights where he shat through three pull-ups. She needed to ask someone here to buy more—ask politely and pretend like she had zero dollars, otherwise they might want her to contribute her last seventeen toward a pack of pull-ups that would cost at least twenty-five, depending on the store.

She yawned. "Let's go, little dolphin."

Out in the hall was a girl with half-bleached, half-dark hair, and a guy with a thousand tattoos.

"Hello," Nola said.

The guy squinted at her.

"Hi," the girl said, glancing at James, who had stomped over to the houseplants by the front door. "Anyway, I don't think that's a valid argument, because . . ." and they kept on walking down the hall. Did they live here? But they weren't old. Must be visiting. Unless maybe they were dying early and had moved here to be among others who were dying, too.

Vara in her wheelchair came around the corner and said, "Sweetie, let's get you up to bed."

"No but."

"I can keep him company while you sleep. He'll be fine."

"It's just," Nola said, looking at James, who was slapping his palms on the wall, "he can get pretty loud? He doesn't mean to be annoying, but . . ." She was apologizing, which she wasn't supposed to do. *Never apologize, never explain—you don't owe them shit.* But if Stell herself had apologized once in a while, she might have been able to keep Nola and James, and she wouldn't be paying fines to CPS for their expenses while they were in care, and Nola and James wouldn't be here in this cold old place filled with people getting ready to die.

"I can handle loud," Vara said.

"If he needs to be changed, the bag—"

"I know where the bag is. You just sleep for a while. Then you can eat lunch and watch some TV."

"James won't want to watch TV."

"We'll find something else for him. It's a big house."

Nola pressed her shoulder against her own mouth, so that Vara would think she was hiding a yawn.

"You look slammed," Vara said. "There's a bed on the third floor. We'll take the elevator. Did you know there's an elevator? And don't worry about the stuff on the walls, that's coming off soon, but for now it'll make the room nice and quiet."

"Is it a padded room?"

"Oh, sweetie, no! It's just a regular one with soundproofing."

Upstairs, in a room with black foam all over the walls, Vara asked: "Do you take care of James a lot at your aunt's house?"

Nola shrugged, sitting tight-kneed on the twin bed, wishing everyone would go away.

"What sorts of things do you do with him?"

"Walk him home from school and give him snack and sometimes dinner, depending which bus Stell gets. Then she does his teeth, medications, bath, and story."

Or: used to do his teeth. Until she kind of stopped. There was a yellow buildup on his front bottom ones from sleeping with his mouth open. Nola had tried to explain this to the case manager—that it wasn't Stell's fault he slept with his mouth open—but the facts didn't come across how she wanted them to, and the case manager *grew concerned*. But Stell *had* taken him to the dentist. She had! The dentist just couldn't make him keep his mouth open long enough to do a cleaning. It wasn't Stell's fault the dentist sucked.

"The marks on his wrists," Vara said. "How did—"

"At the hotel he wouldn't fall asleep. Sometimes it takes him a long time to fall asleep, even with his meds. He kept running around and freaking out, so they tied him to the bed."

"Why were you at a hotel?"

"It's when they can't find a placement for you. You stay there with CPS caseworkers. There has to be two of them so you can't accuse one of sexual assault." She waited for Vara to say how awful that sounded, to ask about the restraints or the caseworkers or how long they'd been living at the Residence Inn. To her surprise and relief, Vara only nodded.

"Get some rest," Vara said, "and I'll take this gentleman downstairs."

Curled shrimplike under the duvet, Nola went straight to sleep.

Kitchen

"FOR YOU, LITTLE ONE, let's organize a treat."

The treat was gummy bears. James batted the first handful away, ignored the second. He took a whisk out of the dish rack and bounced it lightly against the kitchen table. She put five bears on the table. He eyed them, returned to the whisk-bouncing.

"You might like them."

He might. He might not. He didn't feel ready to try. Maybe he *would* feel ready. Maybe soon. When was soon? And where was Nola? He hit the whisk against the table harder, pulling the heavier sensation into his hand and wrist, up his arm, into his shoulder, across his whole torso, swinging the whisk until its vibration took up every piece of space inside him.

"Okay, now we need toputsomethingonyourwrists." She took hold of his forearm. "This'll make it feel better."

The words *feel better* exasperated him: they always came right before someone shoved a syringeful of medicine in his mouth or pasted a bandage on his skin that he would need to rip off. He didn't want her touching his arm. He wanted his arm to be alone.

"Sweetie, I need todothissoitwontgetinfected."

Leave me alone, his slapping hand said. He scampered away and she said, "Later, then?" and he carried the whisk to the floor by the butcher block. A stream of cold air on his shoulder blades felt like water coming out of the wall.

He decided to climb. Dragged a chair over to the counter.

"Hey, no, come down!" the other one said.

When he felt like it, he would.

"Down, please. You're gonna fall."

He wouldn't fall, he was a careful person, but the other one didn't know this yet. James compromised by sitting on the counter, rather than standing. Where had the whisk gone? He watched the other one take a green bag from the fridge. He dangled one foot until it found the stepstool, planted the other foot alongside it, made sure he had his shoelace, and descended. Where was the whisk? He kicked the pleasingly thick leg of the butcher block.

"Hey James."

He turned.

"Do you like snow? Itmightsnowtomorroweventhoughitsearly intheseason."

He still wanted his whisk. He went over to the sink, where the other one was washing leaves.

"Hungry?"

James knuckle-tapped his chin yes. He would've liked to play with the faucet water, too, but would content himself for now with a leaf from the sink—glossy, red-veined. He tasted the stem: not good, not bad. The leaf part was more interesting to his teeth.

The first one ran her fingers through James's hair, which felt good until it didn't and he twisted away, pressing the crumple of chard to his chest. "You are a *wriggler*, little one," she said.

He was mad at them for not finding the whisk. He shouted his displeasure and they both started talking at him, jangly, which made him angrier.

"Let's try somethingelseforyou," she said. "I'm thinking . . ." Then she was gone, and the whisk was gone, and the other one wasn't helping. James banged on the latticework again.

"Can you do it quieter?" the other one called.

A third person came in, carrying a blue yoga ball. "Look, James! Wanna bounce?"

James did not. He wanted the whisk, which they had not found, so he wasn't staying. He ran out into the hall and down its length until he reached the plants by the door. He touched a drowsy frond of the bamboo palm, tore a shred off the fern. The air was damper close to the pots; it smelled of minerals and rot, of microscopic creatures busy in the soil.

Infirmary

IN THE EARLY SPRING of 1919, it had taken the captain and his young sons most of a day to dig a grave in the near-frozen ground. The daughter watched. The body of their mother lay waiting in a tarpaulin, neatly rolled. There was a ban on public funerals, to slow the spread of the Spanish flu.

After they buried her, the captain had had a recurring dream so persistent and so frightening it flickered here still, in the beams of the House. He was trying to dig the hole with his fingers. His sons had run off with the shovel and spade. His head was crammed with silver, and the silver made its own sound, and the cold ground refused him. Not a dent after clawing and clawing. It should have been too cold for smells, but he could smell meat—the flesh of his wife. Through the tarpaulin. His Adeline who loved clouds, who had named their daughter Ula because it meant jewel of the sea.

THE ROOM IN WHICH THIS DREAM HAD HAPPENED waited now for Vara to unlock it, to roll in and wash her hands and turn the computer on.

The mosquitoes were hatching at higher elevations. Why did her mind cling to it?

She carefully pressed RECORD on her phone and said:

"Chart notes, November first.

"Mr. Rudd presented with UTI again. Problem unclear at first because did not want to disclose. Was angry and ashamed. Quote, The damn stream is splitting. Or sometimes it's just driblets, unquote. Wanted to know if it could be a sign of cancer.

"Caz reported visual disturbance, twenty-five minutes, followed by headache, two hours, and general poor feeling. No nausea. Daily caffeine intake less than eight hundred milligrams. Elevated anxiety levels. BP one thirty-nine over eighty-nine. Admin Excedrin four hundred milligrams.

"Finally managed to get some calendula on James's welts. Also five-millimeter cut on his right index finger, superficial. Iodine on wound, tried a Band-Aid but he keeps pulling it off. My lord, what a cutie. Gives you this secret sideways look."

Vara sprayed disinfectant at the counter. Puff, wipe. *You would've made a fine doctor*, she used to be told. Puff, puff, wipe, wipe. Her hands ached. She'd never met a doctor she liked. Most were unbearable people. Barely people. The room needed mopping, but Ant was too busy with their dissertation. Was that blood on the floor? A dark smear. Dried, at least. In nursing school, other students had been bothered by things that didn't bother Vara at all—ablative procedures, defunctive smells. A short film on nystagmus had given one classmate a panic attack.

Gloves. Pink tray. Into plastic cups went the capsules and tablets. They were getting low on Davey's extended-release bupropion.

Caz, from the doorway: "Trick or treat! Trick or treat!"

"The bitter and the sweet," Vara answered, rubbing the coarse tread of her chair's right wheel.

"I'm heading to school—I can't access the database from here. You okay keeping an eye on the kids?"

"They won't think it's strange you're showing up on a day off?"

"Oh, nobody cares. I'll just pop on the computer and get James's mom's number."

"Call her from one of the school phones," Vara said, "not your cell. Once the kids are reported missing, they'll put surveillance on her."

"Um, this isn't *Midsomer Murders.*"

"Just in case."

"It hasn't even been twenty-four hours. And it could've been a foster family who did that to James, not the caseworkers. Maybe the kids were at the hotel for their own safety."

"You think Nola's lying?"

"I wouldn't blame her. She probably just wanted to get out of there. I'll talk to Stell and see what she wants us to do."

"Why did she lose custody?" Vara said.

"What are you, chief of the virtue police?"

"It's a relevant question, I think."

"I have no idea," Caz said. "She's a good mother."

Vara felt her face heat up. "*Good mother* is a bullshit term."

"But you know what I mean."

"It's a marketing ploy."

"Fine, then," Caz said, "she's . . . a decent person."

"How do you know?"

"Because I have talked to her, lots of times. At pickup, you know, and parent/teacher night type of shit." Caz took off her glasses, breathed on the lenses, and wiped the condensation with her sweatshirt sleeve. "Regardless, I'm definitely calling her before I call anyone else."

"I just don't want you getting in trouble."

"Well, I won't. Fear of failure, fear of reprimand."

"Two big problems I never had," Vara finished, with the old scratch of envy. Those lyrics were sometimes true for Caz, but they'd never applied to her.

Front Hall

"HELLO," SAID THE ONE with the scraped-velvet voice.

James looked up at her—not far, she wasn't much taller—then back at his shoelace.

"Does that leaf taste good?" she said.

Her body was tiny and electricity poured from her dark little eyes. She had a smile that resembled his mama's, but her voice was lower and had scars that clicked. Scraped places. His mama was soft and big and loved him forever plus three minutes. Billy goats gruff, brothers three. *Who's that trip-trapping over my bridge?* Mama did the troll's voice with no scrapes. When could he be with her? Soon! she'd said last time. Soon, little bear. But when was soon?

He stomped hard with one foot for the pleasure of feeling the floor.

"Well, Iwillleaveyoutoit," she said.

He had ripped a long ringlet off the fern and was considering its taste, which didn't please him. Too crackly. He dropped the fern and twirled his shoelace. His eyes wanted the motion of his dancing hand. Nobody here had tried—yet—to make him stop moving his hands. He wanted Mama to squirt strawberry bubbles into his bath, Mama to wrap him tight in the striped towel, Mama to pull back the bedcovers ("Pop in, little fin") and tuck them firmly around him. *All was quiet in the deep dark wood. The mouse found a nut and the nut was good.* When would he see her? When was soon? He hated not knowing, *hated* it, and was furious at Nola for not knowing either; or, if she knew, not telling him. But he didn't think she knew.

Dining Room

HIGH CEILINGS, GREEN WALLS, round tables, weird smell. Stupefied from the nap, Nola was answering Vara's questions less politely than she usually would have.

"And you were both living with James's mother?"

"Yeah, my aunt Stell."

"Was it just the three of you?"

"Yeah."

"And how was that?"

"Fine. Good."

"Would James like a whole-wheat scone, do you think?"

Nola shrugged.

"James, do you want this?" Vara held out the scone, which he ignored, instead running to a window and banging on the pane.

"He might not be hungry, he ate a lot of crackers before."

"That's fine," Vara said, watching him wrap himself in the mustard-colored curtain.

"Could I have it, though?"

"Oh, of course! Sorry." Vara set it in front of Nola. "How long have you been—away from your aunt?"

"A while," Nola said. *Need-to-know basis* was one of Stell's rules. She watched Vara think about pressing for more. The scone was dry as hell. Would they notice James's teeth?

"What kinds of things does James like to do?"

"Go to Safeway."

"Okay. What else?"

"And the McDonald's drive-through."

"I mean, what does he like to play with? What kinds of toys?"

Nola yawned. "He likes to hang out."

"What about you?"

"What toys do I play with?"

"Well, more as in—what do you like? Books? Movies? When my daughter was your age, she loved to draw."

"I'm an avid reader," Nola said. This was not true, but adults tended to relax when they heard it.

"Oh, do you know"—and she said the title of a book Nola's teacher had read aloud to them last year, which was narrated by a ten-year-old with a photographic memory who solved a mystery while using long vocabulary words. This kid was nothing like Nola, nothing like James. If Nola ever wrote a book, it would star a protagonist who was *not* gifted. Someone who made mistakes and didn't learn from them.

"There she is! Hey, Miss Nola." Caz sat down next to her. "How're you doing? How's James managing?"

Nola heard in her voice the over-niceness that often precedes disappointment. She held in her stomach so that her body wouldn't move if there was bad news. "Fine, thank you."

Fiddling with the remains of the scone, Caz said, "So, here's the deal. I talked to James's mom."

"Okay."

"She'll come get you tomorrow," Caz said. "Her car's in the shop. She'll pick it up in the morning. So you guys will stay here tonight, yeah?"

Need-to-know basis. There was no reason for Caz to know that Stell didn't have a car. Nola kept her smile small, but the relief was massive. Her own part was done. Stell could take over now. And yet, Stell didn't have a car.

"My cousin's gonna run out of diapers soon," she said.

"Oh. Okay." Caz looked stumped.

"Davey can buy some on his way home from work," Vara said.

"Thank you. Pull-ups, size M. They're in the baby aisle but they're not regular diapers."

Caz pulled out her phone. "I'll text him."

"Also I couldn't bring his medications, and he'll need them tonight."

"What does he take?"

"Point five milligram risperidone, point two milligram clonidine, one milligram lorazepam."

"I don't have risperidone in stock," Vara said. "The other two, yes."

James's meds were in the bag with their toothbrushes—they were the first thing Nola had packed—but they might as well get some for free.

"It won't hurt him to miss a dose or two," Vara said. "I don't think there's a risk of withdrawal symptoms from risperidone."

"He won't swallow pills, though. You'll have to dissolve them and use an oral syringe."

Vara smiled. "I can do that. I'm an actual nurse, you know."

"Ghee-ah ghee-ah ghee-ah!" James called from his post by the kitchen doors.

"Are you stoked to skip school?" Caz said.

"I guess." Nola's absences were piling up. She was almost fourteen but still in seventh grade because she had missed so many days of fifth they made her repeat it. Her first time through fifth was the year her mother had gone away and Stell became her guardian.

"What about James? You think he'll mind missing a day?"

"Definitely not."

James went to the Resource room, which had kids from all the grades and wasn't in the same building as the regular classrooms. It was in a white trailer by the soccer field. Once, when he kept yelling and trying to leave the trailer, Nola had been summoned to the school office to calm him down. She had heard the principal and James's teacher talking on the other side of the door. "They expect us to work miracles. What are we, a magic compost pile?" Nola had stared out the window at the soccer field circled by the spongy red track where, after rainstorms, tiny penises lay scattered, all the worms come out to drink.

James padded over to lean against Nola's shoulder, twirling his shoelace.

"Hey, buddy, how's it going?" Caz said.

"Mama," James said.

"We'll be with her soon," Nola said, mechanically.

THE MUNICIPAL ELEVATOR in town did not technically need someone to operate it, but the job existed—a pity job, as Davey saw it, arranged by the VA, a government bone for any vet who could press UP and DOWN. Nevertheless, he got spruced for it. Hair combed, shirt with buttons, work boots instead of the shower slides. He lowered himself stiffly into the sixteen-year-old Spectra that was his most faithful companion, the car he'd slept in for weeks after the hospital until his patient advocate told him about the House. Now it took him to work every Friday and also, whenever he felt skittery, along the cliff road above the river, just driving and driving. He and Caz hadn't fucked in it—yet.

The town was split into Upper and Lower. On the bluff were chain stores and drive-throughs and houses; down along the riverbank were bars, coffee shops, a small regional museum. The municipal elevator had been built to join the two parts. The town didn't get many tourists, but the ones who did come, the fanny-packed couples from neighboring states, wanted to ride the elevator. In the observation deck at the top, educational posters told of Area Points of Interest, one of which was Davey's own home. He felt proud when he saw people looking at the black-and-white photo of the House from decades ago. *I wake up there every morning!* His lair for now. Maybe even for a while. Actually he could see himself staying forever.

"Is there a security camera on this thing?"

Most of the tourists had the same kind of face: eager and uptight.

"Not that I know of," Davey said.

"Well, there should be." The man crossed his arms and looked at his wife, who nodded in a *You tell him, Brian!* kind of way. "For *your* safety," the man added, "as much as anyone else's."

"I carry a knife at all times."

"Ah, so you're prepared!" the man said, anxious-jolly.

Davey watched their fleece vests and wide, flat butts hurry out onto the observation deck. He used the knife for shaving pills. The 200 mg tabs had a pink coating that smelled disgusting, and the smell didn't totally fade even after the coating was scraped off, but it was less disgusting than if you sniffed the crushed pill unscraped. The coating couldn't legally be poisonous—people swallowed it—although certain substances came up right to the *edge* of poison. The 150 mgs didn't smell. There might have been a 300 but he'd never been prescribed it. When you had DRUG SEEK-ING in your chart it was hard to steer doctors into higher doses, even for antidepressants, which weren't even drugs. He was only drug-seeking compared with, like, Mrs. Quimbee. True addicts OD'd by twenty-seven, and Davey was almost twenty-nine.

He made a list in his mind:

1. Lawn mower
2. Cashier
3. Drayage truck driver
4. Aquarium security officer
5. Soldier
6. Elevator operator
7. Attorney-at-love

Of all his jobs, the aquarium had been the best one. Whenever kids were banging on the tanks, he'd yell, "You break that glass, little octopus gonna run out and kill you!"

Aside from bad-mood Rudd and Adeline who hallucinated black chickens, the people at the House weren't that bad. Caz, obviously, but also the Dragon: all tiny and shriveled yet *fierce*. Nobody fucked with her. She reminded him of his Aunt McClung, who used to sit around in her bathrobe yelling at people. When she'd had some wine she would say, "It's not your fault, David," and he knew she meant his whole life. Last week, when he showed the Dragon his Glock 19, she hadn't batted a single eyelash. Didn't give him any gun-control guff. She'd simply held it in her hands and stared.

Front Yard

SIXTY-TWO FEET FROM THE CAPTAIN'S wife's grave, shivering in her purple windbreaker, Nola stared up at the House. It would have made a decent horror-movie location, the way it leaned all bleak and grim against the tall evergreens, and how the boxy little tower at the top could be a place to keep prisoners. Less horror-movie-ish was the sign sticking up beside the gravel path.

all welcome

όλοι ευπρόσδεκτοι

الجميع مرحب بهم

ongi etorri

onse olandilidwa

都欢迎

zoo siab tos txais txhua leej txhua tus

tena koutou katoa

t'áá ájíłtso hóshdéii'

qof walba waa la soo dhaweyn ayaa

todos bienvenidos

બધંભાવકાર્ય છે

Did *all welcome*, she wondered, have the same meaning in every language? What meaning did it even actually have in English? A washed-out phrase, like *nice to meet you* or *thank you for being a friend*.

James was on the gravel, dancing the shoelace in his fingers, testing the little sharp rocks with his bare toes. The dinosaur skull

T-shirt was too big for him. It was even colder today—she could see goose bumps on his skinny forearms—but he didn't like wearing jackets.

"No more hotel," she told him. "We *hate* the hotel."

He twirled and twirled.

"No more hotels ever," she said, touching his earlobe.

"Ah-eee," James said.

Smelling poop, she pulled at the waistband of his sweatpants to peer inside the diaper. "Okay, bear. We need to change you." She tickled his armpit and he giggled, pushed her away. "Go inside, okay? I'll be there in one minute."

She wouldn't lose him.

But she wanted one minute.

She watched him go into the House. There were too many people in there for him to get up to any true mischief. It wasn't like at home, where, if Stell was at work, anything bad that happened would be Nola's fault.

"Well hi there!" said a voice behind her.

It was a man so handsome he could've been an actor. Salt-and-pepper hair short on the sides, ragged-long on top; silver hoop earrings; tight black sweater. His smile was packed with enormous white teeth.

"I'm a neighbor," he said.

"Okay," she said.

"You know that church up the road? I'm Pastor Jeff. What's your name?"

"Dorothy," she said.

He was carrying a tote bag that proclaimed: Boldly Inclusive. Joyfully Christian. Your Best Life.

"Well it's nice to meet you, Dorothy. Are you visiting one of the residents?"

"Are you a pastor as in you do sermons?"

"That I am, that I am." His gaze flicked to the House, then back to Nola. "You're invited to come hear me on Sunday, if you're still visiting."

"Okay," she said. He might be a pervert.

"Hey, hey, hello!" Lasko came running down the asphalt path. "Time to go inside." He put his palm on Nola's head. "You head on in, all right? Marika needs you for something." To the pastor he said, "This is Marika's great-granddaughter."

"Dorothy," Nola added loudly.

"I didn't know Ms. Dragoumanos had family."

"Go inside, okay, Dorothy?" Lasko widened his eyes at Nola, just the tiniest bit, and it delighted her to share this moment of deception with him, to belong to a household that protected its facts.

Library

HER COUSIN WAS LYING on his belly on the leather couch. "Time to change you," Nola said, but instead of heading for the bathroom, she went to the window. Only the upper part was stained glass; you could see through the lower part into the front yard. The pastor was holding out his tote bag, and Lasko, arms crossed, was shaking his head.

Dorothy Dragoumanos, she thought, was a fire name.

Before the Residence Inn, she and James had stayed at two placements—the nice house and the TV house. According to the oldest boy at the TV house, who had lived with eleven families, a lot of people who fostered were religious. (That boy left soon after Nola and James got there, hauled away by a caseworker after he'd unwrapped every tampon in the box and inserted one into the cat's butt.) At the nice house, the parents had been young and gentle and prayed before every meal, at every bedtime. The mother made blueberry waffles on the weekends. James was "too much" for them. *We just can't give him what he needs, I'm sorry, he's a sweet boy but way too much for us to handle, I'm so sorry.*

James went to stand with Nola at the window. He looked at the gold heaped and scrunched on branches. Red berries clustered. Plump lime-yellow leaves with one stark vein through each middle. Brown shadows crinkling on the gravel, on the grass, on the dirt where the grass stopped. Shaggy cones of green pointing softly at the sky.

Kitchen

"IT DOESN'T SOUND LIKE a good idea," Vara said.

"Not to *you*," Caz said, "because you are doom-prone. It seems logical to me."

"Me too," Lasko said. "Like, if your kids are in danger, you get them out of danger."

"Exactly."

"Why doesn't she just file a complaint about the caseworkers," Vara said, "and the kids would be reassigned, and she wouldn't risk being arrested for child abduction?"

"She *did* complain. Last week. But that's not even the main problem. Something about James getting sent—somewhere? She didn't give me details. Whatever it was, she said she couldn't let it happen and she had to get the kids out of there and as soon as her car is ready, she'll come get them."

"They're saying flurries tomorrow," Vara said.

"Already? Fuck."

"We've got a few bags of snow-melt left over from last year," Lasko said, scanning the counters for what to clean next, though it was his morning off. "I think the kids should stay as long as they need to. Our House is about radical hospitality, right?"

"Well," Caz said, "semiradical, at least."

TWO DECADES AGO, after she stopped playing music, Caz had lived alone above a Cretan restaurant in Queens. She worked as a substitute teacher and did drugs and spent a lot of time watching people on the subway. Hundreds of thousands of people rode the New York City subway by themselves every day, but Caz did not see them; she only saw the people who rode with other people. Lovers, families, coworkers, friends. They smiled and yawned and rooted in shopping bags and held hands. She collected their shards of conversation and was embarrassed by how much she wanted someone to talk to, even if just about songs or the weather.

One morning she took two trains and one bus to reach a school in Brooklyn that smelled like gasoline. A line of first graders marched in at nine o'clock. One girl asked, "Will we make planets?" "Why not," Caz said. They knew where the paper was. The girl drove her crayon around the page. Messy dark hair and a mermaid barrette. She told a kid not to keep bumping her elbow. "Do you know what color is Saturn?" Caz did not. "There's no air on Saturn so you can't live there." "Yeah but what about you could be hooked up to a tank," the elbow bumper said. "I'm gonna run to the bathroom," Caz said, "don't attack each other." They stared back from small faces. On the bathroom door was a paper sign dangling on nailed yarn. Green side GO, red side STOP.

She forgot to turn it to STOP.

They brought in a guidance counselor from another school, since that school didn't have one, to talk to the mermaid-barrette girl. She kept saying *the dead teacher* even after the counselor explained Caz had not died. These facts were typed in a letter from the principal explaining that he would not press charges if she went to rehab. If she had flipped the sign to stop, the girl's brain would not be scratched forever with Caz's blue face and the needle hanging off her arm and blood on the floor from earlier tries. The girl had run down the gasoline-smelling hall to the school office yelling, "Teacher's dead!"

When they pulled out the tube it tore the walls of Caz's throat. Stunned on the stretcher, afraid they would yell at her again, she tried to taste what was wrong with her tongue. "Why're you crying, bitch?" It killed to swallow. The ambulance ceiling shuddered when they hit potholes. She stared at the ceiling and the bright bars of wet light. Hands on her chest when she tried getting up. "Settle down." The lights leaking purple and yellow. "What the fuck are you crying for." Her mouth didn't work, couldn't get enough air, she had to keep gulping to start her own breath. Her throat walls felt sanded to blood. The medics didn't like her because it was her own fault, she was taking up precious time on their stretcher, there were other people to save that day who had not caused the emergency themselves.

A week after finishing in-patient treatment in Minneapolis, Caz relapsed and went back to in-patient then spent four months at a St. Paul halfway house called Tranquility Lodge. Everyone at the Lodge wanted to be worse-than. They bragged about cutting, slicing, shooting—the thousand ways they had hurt themselves: the bigger the pain, the bigger the respect. Ever suck cock for it? Wake up in a pillow of blood because your gums were melting off from it? Did you ever get a drip of medicine sewn into your stomach to stop you from getting high, then rip the stitches open and yank it out?

Threatened with expulsion unless she found a job, Caz applied at the car wash that hired residents of Tranquility Lodge because its owner was a recovering crack addict. She was given a red bandanna to tie back her hair and assigned to the easiest spot on the line: taping rear wipers to windshields. I should not be working at a car wash, her mind said. Her mind wanted everyone to understand that she should not be working at a car wash, that she'd once stood on stages, that her name meant something to people who knew about music.

A fellow resident said, "Can we do a dyadic encounter later? I need one more for the week."

"Just write fake answers and put my name on it."

"Not my first rodeo. This time it has to work. So I'm doing my dyadics."

This Lodger, whose job at the car wash was to guide each customer until their wheels caught on the conveyor track, was mildly hot. He had amazing shoulders. Caz sucked in her stomach, sausagey in the jeans that had been loose a month ago, and shrugged. "If you want."

"Thanks, man." He started to clap Caz on the back, but his hand stopped mid-arc.

That night they sat on the front porch in the bright, deep cold. A car turned onto the avenue and sped past, its driver a citizen of the regular world. They lived on the ship of the Lodge, sealed off, shut in. From its deck they watched the snow crusting into hard blue surges and the black arms of trees and a restaurant sign glowing valentine-red. Where were you born? What's your favorite food? What would you bring to a desert island? Name one of your most significant life goals.

The other Lodger's goal was unsupervised visits with his kids. Caz's was a job that wasn't the car wash. She began, to her horror, to cry. The face-clenched, spasmodic kind of crying.

"Aw, hey, Hamburglar! You're only, what, thirty—?"

"Forty-two."

"You'll goal up soon."

Nodding, sniffling, Caz lit a new cigarette from the cherry of the old.

"Crying's good. It releases the toxins."

"That's a myth," Caz said, though she knew nothing whatsoever about it.

What if she never experienced any desires beyond the physical, the immediate? What if she was actually—

"Would you rather swim in a forest lake or an indoor pool?"

—shallow?

"That is literally the most irrelevant question I have ever been asked," Caz said. Her hands were so cold. The restaurant sign flickered, went dark.

"Lake or pool?"

"I'm a loose fleck."

"What?"

"Of garbage."

Frowning, the fellow resident looked at his wrist, where there had once been a watch.

"I have no function, when you think about it. Like, at all?" Caz shoved her aching hands between her thighs.

"Be well," the amazing-shouldered guy said and headed into the house, not slowly.

At lunch the heir to a timber fortune told her: "You're going to gain so much weight here you'll have to wear sweatpants. Did you bring any?" Rolls at every meal, cheap ones. Caz loved their chewy middles that were never cooked all the way through. The bread grew in layers on her arms; she watched the track marks fade. The timber heir's tracks were worse than Caz's. He wore fray-strapped halter tops and a jean jacket with threads dangling from the back where he'd pulled off band patches. His face was a lace of scabs. You didn't notice at first but closer up you could see the gashed grooves, capped with hard new shells of skin.

It didn't take long on halfway-house time to become somebody's sister. You smoked and ate sugar and smoked and drank coffee and smoked together, got so bored you want to kill someone together. Caz had gone from hating the sight of the heir to looking for his scabby face first in a room, running to sit beside him. She went back to hating him again and then not, and then hating again, and then again not because she might as well have been his sister, thick as thieves the two of them were. The other Lodgers asked, "Are you sleeping together?" and the heir yelled, "I'm a fag, motherfuckers!" and Caz didn't tell him about her dead best friend West because he might think she wanted him to be West's replacement, which she secretly sort of did.

Caz got off work an hour before the heir. She'd wait on the porch for him to come trudging down the street in his milk-stained Pony Espresso shirt. The heir disliked the job but couldn't complain, because one complaint from someone who was known to be rich and the other Lodgers would annihilate him. He held out a frosted heart.

"Want this?"

"What flavor is it?"

"Corporate Baked Good flavor."

Caz ate it, and he finished her cigarette, and they watched a small cloud puff along behind the church steeple. I am happy, her mind said. They cooked your meals, told you what time to wake up, gave you fresh sheets and a new little soap every Monday. People asked how you were feeling and never scorned you for feeling bad, for having trouble living in the world, because everyone at the Lodge had this trouble. You talked to whoever sat by you at dinner or stood smoking on the same porch you were standing on. You could ask questions too intrusive, and hear answers too revealing, for the regular world. *My husband gave me gonorrhea. When I was nineteen I killed a field hockey coach in a DUI.* Then you were free to drift away to your room, or it would be time for the next meal, or another resident would barge into the conversation. No danger of being stuck across a café table trying to come up with things to say and wondering how much more time had to pass before you could leave. When you met someone for coffee in the regular world, you were expected to stay an hour at least; but what about the people you only had half an hour's worth of talk for? Ten minutes' worth? *Five* minutes? Caz enjoyed many good five-minute exchanges at the Lodge. Crunched together for months on end, you felt affection, even love, for people you barely knew. Others who had come to scoff but remained to pray.

It was this feeling—the happiness of accidental, sideways, all-comers kinship—she had hoped to replicate when she started the House.

Dining Room

FOR DINNER THERE WAS beef brisket, green salad, and new bread. Everyone sat at one of the two round tables except Marika, who had dragged a chair to the little dropleaf under the clock.

"Impossible to know," Mrs. Quimbee said, "what that smug platypus is thinking. She likes to laugh into her own little cup of darkness."

"She *can* be sociable," Kestrel said, "she just—"

"Sociable as a Swiss bidet! I don't think she wears deodorant."

"The fuck is a bidet?" Davey said.

"Washes the nether-parts."

"What, like a crotch servant?"

"It's an appliance," Mrs. Quimbee said. "Go anywhere in Western Europe, there will be one next to the toilet."

"Okay, I'll just go anywhere in Western Europe on my salary of eighty-four dollars a month."

"You have a job?"

"I work for the state," he said.

"If operating an elevator once a week," Kestrel said, "counts as working for the state."

Davey narrowed his eyes and scraped his front teeth with a spoon. "More if somebody calls out sick."

"Don't you get money from the government?"

"Yeah, Vera, us vets are living massive on our money from the government. We are so well tooken care of by the government."

"It's *Vara*, and I only meant—"

"That's why we're all killing ourselves."

"Huh?"

"They ought to make the Dragon wear deodorant," Mrs. Quimbee said.

Marika could hear every word. She took the tissue wad from her dress sleeve. One of these days Mrs. Quimbee must be made to shut up.

"Davey sacrificed for our country," Kestrel said.

"He was a wage-earning assassin," Vara said, "with health insurance. There's no draft. Why should we revere boys who choose to get paid to kill people?"

Davey, grinning, slammed down the spoon. "Butter my nut and holler my name!" When it was only robots and drones fighting the wars, he thought, what were they going to do with the human leftovers? Were there enough aquarium-security jobs in America?

The German soldier who had killed Marika's brother had been even younger than Davey. His hair was reddish, the soldier's, and his ears stuck straight out. "Stand up, Jew!" he'd said in Greek, and when her brother didn't, he shot him dead.

"Why don't we do another community question," Mrs. Quimbee said. "I will begin. What is a memorable anecdote you remember about a friend?"

"I just fell asleep because that question is so boring," Kestrel said.

"Guess what, you vehement onion—"

"I had a friend at the VA," Davey said. "This junkie kid. He'd been at it so chronic he burned out all the usual pipes, right, and one day he jacks into a hand artery and his hand blows up to five times the size and he comes into the hospital and they put him under and when he wakes up, the hand is gone."

"Gone where?" Kestrel said.

"They cut it off. Because it died."

"How does a hand die?" Mrs. Quimbee said.

"It just does."

"But what does that *mean*?"

"I don't know, the nerves, like, shrivel? He was funny, that kid. I forget his name." Davey stood up from the table. "I need to go take a dump."

At the table closer to the kitchen doors, James pushed away the plate Lasko had made for him and tapped his cousin's wrist.

"He isn't going to eat this," Nola said. "Do you have peanut butter?"

"We can't because," Adeline said.

"Of the Dragon," Rudd finished.

Peanuts were wood-colored meat in flimsy jackets. The first handful she ever tasted, in 1945, at the Feldafing camp for displaced persons, had made Marika stop breathing. They'd had to dump cold water on her face, buckets and buckets, until she started again. She still hated the sight of a peanut or its butter, but if this little one wanted it, she would make a hundred sandwiches for him. Peanut butter and honey and good thick bread. The previous cook here had stuck to machine loaves in orange bags; Lasko baked it fresh. Bread, bread, bread, forget them! *I am hungry* had been the first English sentence she learned at the Feldafing camp.

"No peanut butter," Rudd whispered, "no tomatoes, no pleasure at all. My daughter is a solicitor and would be interested to hear what goes on here."

The boy was yelling and pulling on the girl's arm. She started to sing to him: "There were six in the bed and the little one said, 'Roll over. Roll over.' So they all rolled over and one fell out . . ."

Marika went over and squatted in front of James and took one of his bare feet in her hands. He kept still for a moment—staring at her hands, then into her eyes—before he was off again, running for the windows.

Rudd watched the girl. One eye on her food, the other on the little boy. Pink barrettes in her dull-colored hair like the ones his daughter used to have. After the gormless cow had thrown him out, he lived in a room too small for Georgina to stay overnight. He'd seen her on Wednesday and Saturday afternoons. A crap way of being a dad. Chicken pot pie after chicken pot pie. The girl became polite with him. When his ex moved to the States, Rudd had followed, because otherwise he might have stopped having a daughter.

"Some bread, then?" Nola said. "He likes apples, too."

Lasko nodded, wiped his mouth with a napkin, and stood.

"You sit," Marika said. "I'll get it."

"You sure, Ms. Dragon?"

"I am very sure," she said.

THE HOUSE'S FOOTPRINT was sixteen hundred square feet, not counting the tunnel. It had a cedar shingle roof, timber-framed lath and plaster walls, and a broad skylight on the ceiling of the main room. This skylight had been the first instruction the sea captain gave to the builder. He'd wanted the room to be octagonal in honor of the cephalopod, and glass-roofed in honor of his wife. And a library: what was the best tree for bookshelves? The captain carved ELKARREKIN into a piece of scrap wood and nailed it to the cladding above the front door. On learning this word, years earlier, in the port of Bilbao, he'd thought his wife would be interested in its angles and repetitions. The new house was for her, for Adeline, his word-loving, cloud-loving, dead wife. The captain insisted that his own bedroom face north, even though the builder kept saying north was bad for bedrooms, being the coldest direction; and he wanted exactly one hundred and twenty-four feet between the house and her grave.

First it had been a house, then a convalescent home for soldiers, then a house again, then a bed and breakfast called the Brizo Inn, named after the schooner *Brizo*, the captain's first command. Iron-hulled, three-masted, a hundred and twenty-four feet long. He had wanted to christen his daughter Brizo, but his Adeline had insisted on giving her a softer-sounding nautical name. To Ula and her brothers, at bedtime, the captain sang a song about a corpse who becomes a mermaid who wanders the ocean for years before walking back onto land as the once-dead woman, alive again and desperate to reunite with her husband. Although he had composed

"Up from the Glad Brine" himself, he told the children it was a famous traditional shanty. "Now she haunts the harbor," he sang, "she who breathes again." The children pretended to believe it was a famous traditional shanty.

Now other children slept here. But they weren't sleeping yet. In Ula's room, on the bed, Nola sat with her arms wrapped around her knees, rocking back and forth. In Ula's brother's room, most recently occupied by the anti-cement activist, James was singing, and Marika was listening. She had volunteered to stay with him until he fell asleep.

Third-Floor Hall

NOLA NEEDED TO PEE. Dim from one tiny lamp, the hallway was a tunnel of black flowers. She never would have chosen this wallpaper, beautiful as it was, for her ideal house because it low-key made her think of girls in old-fashioned times coughing themselves to death. She might be having cramps. She hadn't been getting her period long enough to reliably distinguish between cramps and just general negative sensation in that area. She didn't have anything with her and didn't want to have to ask. Diapers were matter-of-fact, an everyday requirement for James, whereas bringing up the subject of her own blood—

She stepped uncertainly down the hall. Every closed door looked equally possible and impossible, then one opened and Kestrel came out in a short yellow robe. Nola asked about the bathroom and Kestrel said she was heading there now and Nola forced herself to ask if Kestrel had an extra tampon and maybe some aspirin and Kestrel said yes totally and started railing against the need to pay for menstrual products that should absolutely freaking be free.

"Toilet paper's not free," Nola pointed out.

"But we *all* share the burden of buying toilet paper."

Nola was too scared of getting full-on, all-out, want-to-die cramps to think about it.

"Follow me," Kestrel said. "This bathroom is sort of frustrating in that the toilet runs constantly? Okay let's see. You probably want a regular, not a super? And you know how to use these, right? It's kind of hard to show someone how to put in a tampon."

Nola laughed because Kestrel was laughing, and said, "There's room on the broom."

"Oh I *love* that, like what the fuck does that even mean? You're so cute. Can I officially appoint you as my little sister?"

"Okay."

Kestrel seemed fake. The fake ones, to get you to like them, acted more caring than the honest ones. "You said you had aspirin, too?"

"Uh-*umm*? Yes! Totally. It's somewhere. Hold on. Fuck. No, I do have some. Here you go, sister."

"Do you mind if I ask why you live here?" Nola said.

"Student-loan debt. Of which I have a shit ton. I don't have to pay rent at the House as long as I hang out with the olds and do chores. It's weird, but I legit love living here. It's like having bonus grandmothers who give you life hacks. For instance, how to not get sick."

"How?"

"Make sure your feet are never cold."

"So I could live here for free?"

"Well, not *you*, necessarily. I don't think the policy includes kids?" Kestrel stared into the mirror, pulling at her eyelashes. "You're one of Caz's students, yeah? I love her. Definitely the coolest of the flesh waffles. In fact, she transcends the waffle category, even if she's old. Did you know that she and Vara were in a band in the late seventies, early eighties?"

"Yeah," Nola said. "My mom liked them."

"I'd never heard of them but Lasko says they're historically significant. Caz wears some of the same clothes, as in literally the same ones, she wore in her heyday. She has this green vinyl jacket I covet."

After Kestrel had peed (not seeming to care that Nola was standing two feet away) and departed, Nola pulled down her sweatpants. Still no blood. She wished her aunt were here to ask about it; in her calm moments, Stell was the best person to consult about most things. In her uncalm moments—Nola pictured her rage-crying when the caseworker said, "If you don't feel guilty, you're not doing it right. It's the parents who don't feel guilty that we worry about." Through snot and tears Stell had screamed that she wanted to know why society was set up this way. Why did guilt and isolation earn you gold stars? Why wasn't anyone actually *helping* them?

Soundproofed Room

MARIKA WAS SNORING beside him. The room was dark. The air on his face was cold. James loved the air in the House, sharp and clean and dry. Where was Nola? Untangling himself from the covers, he sat up. Now his whole body was colder, which made him so happy he punched—lightly—Marika's shoulder. She grunted. He rested his cheek on her small, mounded form, relaxing with the certainty that Nola would come in soon to change him.

Instead of school he wanted to go to Safeway and roam the wide, shining aisles. Touch the steel circles on the floor. Rip a leaf of lettuce from a head on the shelf and chew it. Hang on to the cart while his mama steered until he didn't want to hang on anymore. Safeway was so much better than school that he laughed to think of it, this magnificent stretch of betterness—the pleasure of the vegetables being exactly where they were, of the pizza slices waiting under their little lamp. He twirled the shoelace, excited, maybe they could go today, maybe Nola would take him since Mama was at home. His anger clicked back up: that Nola had kept them away from home so horribly long—first at the loud house, then at the hotel, now here. Why, Nola? his yelp meant.

At the sound, Marika stirred again. He draped an arm across her neck.

"Hey," she said, "I need to breathe, you know."

He wanted to make sure he didn't have to go to school today. The boy who pushed and the girl who screamed got on his nerves, and the teacher didn't know how to use his word device, kept doing the buttons wrong, fumbling so long he would forget what he'd been trying to say.

His eyes felt thick, hardening.

Safeway or school: would Marika tell him? Would Nola? Someone needed to. Mama would have. The mouse found a nut and the nut was good.

Marika's papery hand on his cheek. "Good morning."

She was not going to tell him.

He danced the lace faster in his fingers, faster and faster and faster in front of his eyes until his eyes were soft again. At the window he put his nose against the glass, which was beautifully cold, then drew away and saw the new consistency of the air: quick and blurred and sputtering white. The changed air was leaving itself on the tree branches.

"Would you look at that, little apple," Marika said. "It's snowing."

Ula's Room

NOLA WOKE DISORIENTED, frowning at the light-blue walls, the swooped curtains; then she remembered.

So many other people lived here that someone might have changed the boy by now—his diaper was usually fat with poop first thing in the morning—and it made her think of the Golden Girls' house, where there was always someone around to talk to, even if the person insulted you during the conversation. There was always a nest to return to after thrills or heartbreak, even if the furniture seemed super uncomfortable. Out on the lanai you could nap, grill steaks, or sit wistfully under moonlight, secure in the knowledge that you were not the only one. That was a TV show, not life, obviously. Nola didn't think life could really be like television, but she did think television helped you get through life. It was what you did when you didn't know what to say or how to be. It was Stell having a laugh attack when Sophia said "Maybe that cheap toupee you're wearing retains heat" and rolling from the couch to the floor and James climbing on her back to help her laugh more.

Stell and her sister—Nola's mother—had matching dolphin tattoos on their biceps.

Still do have! Not dead! one side of Nola yelled.

Always remind them you're cousins. They'll be less likely to separate family members. Don't lose him, Nola, whatever happens, you can't lose him, promise me.

They wouldn't have been in this situation if Stell had behaved herself. But it also wasn't really her fault. A different doctor from the one they normally saw had thought the blue birthmark on James's back, which he'd had his whole life, was a bruise, even after Stell explained that it wasn't, and the doctor reported possible abuse to CPS. That, combined with the teeth-brushing problem, combined with the water being shut off due to lack of payment, combined with Stell's bitchiness to the caseworker, had led to their removal.

You can't lose him.

Infirmary

DAVEY CAME TO the door for his morning pills. Vara handed him the little cup. He was quiet today, frowning, scratching forearms swirled thick with spiderwebs and black roses. He didn't say his usual joke about where she kept the good stuff.

"Are you doing okay?" she said.

"Yepper." He nibbled at his thumb.

"Did you see it started to snow?"

"Nope."

"Do you—like snow?"

"I'm indifferent."

He was only a little younger than Vara's son, and his sulky nonanswers irritated her the same way her son's always had. Nepenthe was the mythical drug of forgetting, a remedy this boy could have used. Sorrow exiled. Grief banished. Vara had read his VA file. As much as she judged Caz for sleeping with him, and as much as she didn't want to understand the appeal, she understood the appeal. Davey had beautiful high-slanting cheekbones and his eyes were a color—metallic gray, flecked with yellow—Vara had never seen on a person before, only on cats. Glum beefcake in a Kokopelli T-shirt.

"Well," she said, "I hope you have a nice day."

"Scrotally."

"What?"

"Totally." He loped away.

She pressed RECORD again and said:

"Marika's lesion improving. Inflammation area reduced. VSS. Continue change dressing b.i.d., monitor BP q.d. She is also exhibiting signs of calcium deficiency: muscle cramps in calves, depression, memory loss. She rationalizes the depression—quote, Have you recently looked at the state of the world?, unquote—and won't admit to memory loss, but based on her age, I'm assuming there is some. Resistant to dietary support—quote, I hate milk, unquote. Admin q.d. five hundred milligram calcium and four hundred IU vit D while symptoms persist."

Vara sometimes saw Marika loading her pockets with butters and sugars from the dining room, and Marika saw Vara taking artificial creamers, but they never spoke of it. Marika's eyes were a wet, raisiny brown, her face pale brown and scored with lines, like a walnut shell. Biceps the size of popsicle sticks. She was tiny, but she was tremendous. After coming through a hell no human had been meant to survive, she sat so calmly on that TV couch.

The rising, the warming, the hatching. The world bent on its own destruction.

Caz waltzed into the infirmary without knocking, rubbing her glasses on the hem of her sweatshirt. How many microbes, Vara wondered, was the sweatshirt leaving on the glasses? "Trick or treat! Trick or treat!"

"The bitter and the sweet," Vara answered.

"Fucking snow," Caz said.

"It's beautiful," Vara said.

"But weirdly early. We don't have winter tires on the van yet. Or, like, those things you put over the tires."

"Chains."

"Stell should be here soon—she said between eight and nine. I'll help the kids get their things together after I deal with Adeline."

"Where does she plan to take them?"

Caz shrugged, wrapping a peroxided braid around her finger. "All she said was, 'We'll be good.'"

"Fantastic plan."

"Vara?"

"What."

"Can you please not pour your shit-clouded bathwater over every single thing in the world?"

"The truth does not change according to our ability to stomach it. Have you gotten any responses to the ad?"

"Two ads. One for the CNA and one for the paying resident who will allow us to afford the CNA. And: no." She took off her glasses and closed her eyes. The skin on her face looked dry, halted. For much of her life Caz hadn't had to worry about consequences, because she had avoided the major obligations. Never wanted kids or a house or a full-time job; thought marriage was stupid; declared Vara a traitor when she got engaged. "Is your caring so stifled," she yelled, "so perverted and sick / That you need vows and duties so that it won't slip?" "Yeah, because I'm ideologically unsound," Vara spat back. Caz had RSVP'd yes but spent the wedding day drunk at Coney Island.

Now Caz, who'd once thrown a plastic cup of her own menstrual blood onto the audience from a stage, had a whole houseful of obligations.

Adeline's Room

ACCORDING TO POLLY, the night aide, Adeline had barely slept. She'd kept waking up and shouting and pacing, then at two a.m. insisted on going out to feed the horses. Polly agreed to dress her. They didn't get farther than the kitchen before Adeline remembered the horses were gone.

Now it was eight, and Adeline couldn't keep her eyes open. Caz unhooked her bra and slid the straps off her arms, carefully tugging them through the long cotton sleeves. She could sleep in this shirt, Caz figured—no need to change her into a nightgown. Spike of guilt for taking the shortcut.

Adeline settled herself under the whale quilt. "I saw a black chicken but it was a dog."

Caz brought Tufty the owl from the dresser.

"Now she haunts the harbor," Adeline sang, smoothing Tufty's green nylon hair. "She who breathes again." Her own hair, red and white, drifted against the pillowcase. Caz sat beside her with a bottle of lotion and took time applying it: hands, forearms, neck.

"If it ain't fixed, don't broke it," Adeline said, laughing when her soft underjaw was touched.

"Want me to read to you?"

"No." She burrowed deeper under the covers, and Caz switched off the overhead, leaving the dresser lamp on. "We were there saying come what you are."

"What's that?"

"We were there saying."

"Okay, well, sleep tight."

Adeline rolled onto her side. "You could never control yourself."

"What?"

"The drugs and the noise, and now the cigarettes. Which I smell."

"Don't forget black licorice," Caz said. "Which makes my shit green."

"Oh, Catherine."

"Sorry—*feces*. It makes my feces green."

"Catherine, just stop."

"Sleep well, Mom."

Was Adeline a good mother?

Caz thought of Stell arriving at pickup, in black sweatpants and a jean jacket and bright-red lipstick, frizzy hair flying. The first time they ever talked, more than two years ago, Stell had said, "My sister loved Bolts," and smiled in a way that Caz took to mean *Unlike the other parents, who are too boring to know who you are, I know who you are.* She hadn't pretended to love the band herself, a choice Caz respected. Standing still in the rushing current of kids, Stell had added, "They're not letting James go to music class, because they say he's too disruptive and it's only once a week so what's the big deal, but I think he should fucking be able to go to music class, don't you? Could you help me convince the principal?"

Caz had agreed, embarrassed that it had never occurred to her to wonder about the kids who didn't go to music. Until now she'd only had to deal with parents demanding special treatment for their "gifted" offspring. *She can already play all twelve scales!*

UPON THE SEA captain's death, his sons decided to honor him by creating the Brizo Inn. They renovated the kitchen and added a wing of en suite bedrooms and kicked out their niece, who had been living there with her young daughter.

The winter after Adeline and six-year-old Catherine were expelled from the House, a blizzard broke the skylight, dumping a foot of snow onto the Fish Bowl floor. For hours the Brizo Inn staff had mopped the snow into buckets with not a single guest offering to help. The Inn lasted only a few years, mismanaged into ruin, and the captain's sons spent their remaining days drinking Thunderbird on the ground floor, never bothering to go upstairs.

They died childless, and their sister Ula was already gone, so the House and its three acres passed to Adeline the Second.

She put the property on the market, received no offers that weren't a complete joke, said to hell with it, and for years the House remained an encumbrance, a tax liability hundreds of miles away; until the day, five years ago, when Caz decided to do something with it. Adeline couldn't live by herself anymore. Caz had read about all-ages retirement facilities where rooms were available rent-free to younger people who agreed to spend time with the older residents. Employees lived on site, with meals and housing factored into their compensation. She wouldn't have to care for her mother on her own—other people would be there too, a whole little community. It could be like Tranquility Lodge. Instead of a refuge from drugs and alcohol, it would be a refuge from not having a refuge.

Front Hall

ANT WIPED THEIR SNEAKERS on the mat, wet snow dripping off their parka. The morning walk was the best part of their day, half an hour of quiet motion alone in the forest. They usually steered clear of the road, because they hated seeing that goddamn church, but who needed the road with all this forest?

The front yard had an ADA-compliant concrete path and ALL WELCOME in twelve languages on a wooden sign. Maybe that was true in movie heaven. On actual Earth, some people found themselves a lot more welcome than others.

James was standing by the giant fern, watching Ant.

"Hey, little man."

At this, James gave a cry of protest that rose quickly into a full-on wail.

"What's wrong?" Ant said. "You have a complaint for the management?"

He wailed louder and hit his chin with his fist.

Ant looked closer: his hands were empty. "You're missing your lace, I see." They hung the parka on the coatrack and sat down on the bench and untied one sneaker. "This one's still wet, but it's your only option at the moment." They held out the shoelace and said, "From each according to their ability."

James grabbed the soaked string and whirled around and scampered off.

Dining Room

THE ROOM WORE its original wallpaper, pea-green flock and peeling at the seams. The old windows were out of true. It was warmest at the table near the swinging kitchen doors, where Vara, nauseated, sipped mint tea next to Kestrel, who sipped black coffee.

"You were saying?"

"What was I saying," Kestrel said.

"About your hot bartender?"

"Uhh-*um*? Right—just that she wasn't working the other night. I know her schedule by heart but maybe she was sick. Anyway, I made the trip for nothing. If I had a car, it wouldn't, whatever, but walking all the way to the bus stop is—oh, fuck. Sorry."

"For what?"

"For complaining about a long walk. When—you know. Anyway, but also, Vara, you need to try the pastor's Nia class! It's a very accessible modality. You can do it from your wheelchair."

Vara snorted and swallowed vomit, or the idea of vomit. Nia was for white ladies who liked jazz-handing to elevator funk, but she had to admit that even if the music was terrible, Pastor Jeff did get people to dance. Whether a resident was sitting, standing, or lying down, he would coax a twirl from a finger, a twitch from a hip. Every body had a range of motion, and he found it. Paid no mind to their shame and reluctance. Vara had watched a class or two from the sunroom doorway, aghast at Mr. Rudd's swivels, Mrs. Quimbee's timid shimmy.

"I looked up the pastor's wife," Kestrel went on. "She does a homesteading blog called *Desire to Shine for Jesus*. And she has five kids—three biological, two adopted—and bakes something called apple pandowdy that looks like an untreated skin condition."

"You have a lot of free time," Vara said.

"Not quite as much as you do, since I, at least, work."

"Does having fun on the internet count as working?"

"Sorry, did you mean *being a freelance writer*?"

"Who writes about on-the-go styling gels," Vara said.

"Which are important in the lives of many, as I noted in my recent piece, 'Meet Your New Handbag Hair Hero.'"

"Is that when your hair looks like an old purse? As in, 'Oh no, I woke up with handbag hair'?"

"Negative," Kestrel said. "It's a *hero* for your *hair* that can fit in your *handbag*."

Pulling up beside Vara, Mrs. Quimbee snapped a napkin open across her lap and stared over at the other table. Marika and Nola sat side by side, and James was on the floor at Nola's feet, twirling a shoelace in his fingers. "I didn't think anyone else had grandchildren. Not who visit, at least."

Vara dropped three artificial creamers into her sweater pocket. "Are you feeling a little competitive?"

"I just hope someone plans to give that girl some vitamins. She looks tubercular."

"Mrs. Quimbee," Kestrel said, "how come your wheelchair is so much less fancy than Vara's?"

"I imagine she made out better in her divorce."

"I need a power chair because of my hands." Vara turned to Mrs. Quimbee. "For your information, my ex-husband could barely hold down a job. This chair was paid for by the Icelandic Tourist Board."

"Am I supposed to understand what that means?"

"Well, I'm out." Kestrel stood up. "Always a pleasure, ladies. And remember—" She tapped Vara's shoulder with her phone. "Nia class!"

Mrs. Quimbee pointed to the windows, where fat white flakes were swarming down. "The snow makes me glad."

"On this," Vara said, "we can agree."

Front Hall

THE INCOMING CALL was *unknown*. Caz was no longer afraid of the IRS, so she answered.

"It's Stell. I'm on a pay phone. Can you believe I found a working pay phone? It might be the last one left in America. Anyway: hello."

Was an untraceable call really necessary?

"Hi. I'm about to get the kids ready—they're having breakfast."

"Great. Except I don't have a car yet."

"Oh." Caz stopped walking. She put one finger on the white wall, which had once been papered in blue-and-gold swirls. One of her only memories from living here as a child was that wallpaper, whose swirls she used to stare at until her eyes felt waggly.

"I told you it was in the shop, right, but the actual situation is that I've been trying to borrow a car from James's father, and he's not being cooperative, which is not *surprising* but I was hoping he would get how important this is, which he seems incapable of doing, so I'm wondering, Caz, if you could keep them until I figure out a car. There is no way in fuck I'm letting my little boy go back there."

"Hmm," Caz said.

"He couldn't even do this *one thing* for us, after he's done basically nothing for all of James's life. All he could do was promise not to tell anyone that I asked him. Do you think they could stay until tomorrow? I know it's a lot."

"No, it's fine for another night, but . . ."

A few beats of silence.

Then Stell said, "They're going to send him away on Monday. The caseworker said that the region currently has no available foster families certified for developmental disability, and there aren't any beds in the one residential facility James would qualify for, so they are, quote un-quote, *obligated* to transfer him to a behavioral-health program in another state. She wasn't even sure yet *which* state. That cannot fucking happen. I can't let him be in some random strange place on his own, not knowing why he's there. And what if they leave his diaper unchanged too long and he gets a rash and nobody puts cream on it?"

"Yeah, that can't happen." But what was supposed to happen instead?

"I want to take them to Canada," Stell rushed on. "They have socialized healthcare and James could get more services. And it's colder there, he would love that. Anyway, I'll figure this out, I will somehow find—"

"What about the bus?"

Stell half-laughed. "Little bear on a bus for multiple hours? Massive nightmare."

"You know there's an amber alert out?" The shrill blast from her phone had woken Caz at five a.m.

"Yeah, the cops've already been to my house twice. But nobody's going to look for them at yours. How's James doing?"

"He's good. Always on the move. He seems to like having all this space to run around in."

"Oh, he must be so stoked. He isn't a stay-in-one-room kind of guy. Thank you, Caz—I'm really grateful for this."

Front Yard

MARIKA AND LASKO took James outside. Since he had no shoes, Lasko carried him perched on his hip. James smiled, blinking at the flakes on his eyelashes.

"This one sure loves snow," Lasko said.

Anger pricked Marika's throat. "Don't assume what he loves." Her parents had done the same thing with her brother, making declarations about what Theo liked or disliked that had more to do with how they wanted him to feel than with how he actually felt.

Lasko looked confused, then annoyed. "Maybe relax?" He brushed melting white out of James's hair, which made the boy laugh. "He seems like he's a snow person, is all I'm saying."

Marika was an indoor person. A walk, a swim, God forbid a hike: she had tolerated them in her life, but she was always simply waiting to be home again. She liked kettles and firesides, a covered porch during rain.

"We should ask," she started to say, groping for the name—what was the name? Oh yes! "Caz to make a fire during Community Meeting." The Spanish *casi* from the Greek σχεδόν, which meant in English "almost." Caz had been almost important once, almost well known: a verge person. Kestrel had shown her a grainy video of Caz rolling her eyes back into her head and flailing all over the stage with the microphone while Vara, off to the side, scarcely moving, played a red guitar.

"That would be so cozy. Ouch! No pinching, please."

"We ought to cut his nails," Marika said.

"I know, they're like talons."

"I'll do it, if we can find clippers. Perhaps the infirmary?"

"No, I have some." Lasko rubbed one of James's feet. "Dude, I wish you would at least wear socks! So then, um, if not clippers, what do you use for *your* nails?"

"My teeth," Marika said.

The girl came out onto the path, purple hood pulled tight over her head. Her face wore a quavery, unstable expression Marika couldn't read. Disappointment? Relief?

"My aunt's not coming," Nola said.

"Because of the weather?"

"Because she couldn't get the car." She took James from Lasko and wrapped both arms tight around him and said, "We'll see Mama tomorrow, but not today. One more night."

James struggled to escape, batting at her cheek.

"No hitting," she said.

He yelled and batted harder.

"Stop, bear! Sorry, can you hold him again?"

"Of course." Lasko gathered James back onto his hip.

"Best not to drive on a day like this, anyway," Marika said. "I'm glad you two will be with us a bit longer."

Nola seemed to be weighing the truth of this claim.

Downstairs Bathroom

ONE MORE NIGHT. Then what? Would Stell actually manage to get them to Canada? Could Nola's mother join them in a foreign country if she was on parole? Nola reminded herself not to think that far ahead, because whenever she did, her ribcage and chest felt like someone was sitting on them.

The thing to focus on (she finished wiping James's butt and held the pull-up open for him to step into) was that her cousin wouldn't be sent away. Nola actually liked the main caseworker, who had astrological signs tattooed on her knuckles and always carried chocolate. She was different from the assholes who were with them at the Residence Inn. But the caseworker would have flown back after dropping James off at the facility. Nola's therapist had told her that the CPS computer system hadn't been updated since the 1980s. What if the system lost his information? What if he got trapped somewhere with nobody knowing who his family was?

At their last supervised visit, when the caseworker was in the bathroom, Stell had explained to Nola what to do. She had saved up three days' worth of her anti-anxiety medication, to make James sleep. She had cut leg-holes in her backpack, duct-taped the zipper track to lock it halfway open, and packed a second bag with as many clothes and diapers as she could fit. Then she made the ghost costume out of a hotel bedsheet.

On the first day of music class, Caz had told them that making any kind of art was like being an architect of debris. "The garbage of your life," she said. "You can give it a shape."

Sunroom

RUDD SAT BY THE RADIATOR, notecards and pen in his lap. Every Saturday he wrote to his daughter.

Last week at the old fucks home, oh excuse me, I'm not allowed to call it that, at The Place Where I Live Now, the management brought in some singing schoolchildren to distract us from our ruin. They looked quite thrilled with themselves, doing this favor for a few sacks of rattling skin. Problem #2: the management denies us tomatoes because one person is allergic. Problem #3: one of the residents is unhinged. He cuts his nails into the night snack. I've seen him do it. Straight into the custard. That was no flake of coconut—that was human hoof.

I will ask you again and keep asking: why in God's green fuck did you sign that form, Georgina? Dump old dad in a home—and not even a good home! It's too cold and the hall smells of piss. It would be brilliant if you'd come rescue me. If I have to stay here another month, let alone the rest of, etc., I don't know what. They're giving a bed to every criminal and refugee. Taking overflow from the veterans' hospital. There's one lad covered in spiders. The biddies must wonder if they'll be raped in their rooms. I wouldn't mind if a criminal stole my wallet and hit me a little, in fact hoping one does, elder abuse could be my ticket out. Seeing's how my own daughter won't break me free.

She had visited here once, his Georgie. Came to see (guilty conscience) how he was liking the place. She'd brought his old favorites, strawberry milk and a chicken-and-mushroom slice, and he tore the plastic wrapping with one hand because the other arm was still in a cast from the accident.

"Dad, are you—is that—does it hurt?"

"I've had worse."

"If you really hate it here, I guess we could . . ."

"I'm fine." He swigged the pink milk.

"Really, Dad?"

"Course I am."

"The people seem nice."

Rudd pinched the bridge of his nose. "They do?"

"It seems like you have friends."

"*Friend*'s a strong word."

"You'd be so bored if you lived with us. I'm always at work."

"San fairy Ann, Georgina."

His girl hadn't needed the aggravation. Though the bathroom here smelled awful. Wasn't it illegal for windowless bathrooms not to have fans? Without them, the stink lingered for dangerous lengths of time. The powder room downstairs could be a chamber of horrors, depending how soon on the heels of another you entered it. Rudd himself had bombed that little room. Not his fault there was no fan! Apart from the elevator you'd think the House hadn't been improved one inch from its original condition—the jagged floors, the leaky window frames. It was cheap for good reason. Only the fifth-best for dear old Dad! But solicitors were supposed to be rich. Oh, she had explained it, sure—she was assigned to the clients too poor to pay. Even when she was little, Georgie had felt sorry for every last streak of piss.

This morning he'd been unable to locate his toothpaste.

Someone had been stealing it then returning it to a different spot in the bathroom. The one next door, he wouldn't put it past her. She was like the bride of Frankenstein's granny, all shriveled and gone-eyed, but she could move at a tidy clip; she'd have no trouble getting in and out quickish. Too cheap to buy her own toothpaste. It was important, he thought, to maintain some order, even here. Act like a civilized person. The Dragon was very rude, and so was the Kestrel girl—they were the worst, but there was stiff competition from the biddy Quim.

Pity he'd never been a reader; you could do all of Shakespeare in a week with the empty time here. *If you really hate it*, Georgie had said, but she'd never gone so far as to offer an alternative.

Three times he had fallen because of the hole in the Fish Bowl floor. The falls were more humiliating for him, in his opinion, than they would have been for somcone who'd never heard ten thousand people scream because of what his feet could do with a ball, who had never been uncatchably fast, his blood roaring and his lungs like silver machines. Now the spasms at night. The screechy burn when he peed. The time it took to get up from a chair. But he had once heard the screaming, and he had once been uncatchable.

Georgina, I beg you (he wrote):

REMOVE ME FROM THIS HELL-TROUGH! There's children here again today, one of which is wild and the other of which looks like you at that age.

The shoulder's been worse and I asked nurse for painkiller. They want me to do PT so I can avoid surgery but I can't endure the company of him who poisons the night snack and doesn't believe I was a footballer. Little do he know I once could run. Maximum recorded speed 32.7

kph. Faster than Messi. We're talking dinosaur era, mind. In those days Reading had a goalkeeper named Steve Death. Short as a mushroom, but he was formidable! It broke my heart to hear you didn't like your name. Your first Christmas home from uni you were yelling, "George Best was a desperate drunk and a terrible father!" Well, he was fucking brilliant at the one thing, and how many of us can say the same? You were named for a singular talent. I hope you'd admit I was a better dad than Best, even in the bad years, which, if we're being fair, were half your mother's fault.

Sincerely,

Your Dad

Had he mailed the cards, he would have gotten no answer back. She could be such a bitch, his Georgina.

AS THE SNOW GREW HEAVIER on the roof . . .

The rag rug in the top-floor hall steamed with Fronzi's piss.

Ant in the kitchen was telling Lasko and Kestrel about the battle to unionize grad students at their university.

James in the library was loving the swollen, glossy chair. His fingers ran all over the seat cushion and the buttoned back. He pressed lightly, then hard, then harder.

Marika in the library was watching James.

Nola in the downstairs bathroom was picturing herself and her cousin in matching pink tuxedos, waiting on the front steps of the House to greet Stell when she arrived.

Caz in the upstairs bathroom was tying up a garbage bag full of James's diapers.

Rudd in his bedroom was thinking about how to buy stamps.

Davey in his bedroom was squeezing a blue pom-pom hat left behind on the municipal elevator by a guy who hadn't seemed lice-ridden or sick. He decided that his mother had sent him this hat.

Mrs. Quimbee in the sunroom was playing solitaire on her phone.

Adeline in her bedroom was dreaming of being hideously thirsty and finding a desert oasis where the shade was guarded by gunmen who sold it in slices. The thing about shade was it never stayed long in the same place, and when her slice had moved to the next patch of sand, when she was back again under the terrible sun, they made her pay for a new slice.

Vara, wheeling past the piano, winced with pain when her chair jolted on the gouge mark.

Fish Bowl

WHY HADN'T CAZ FIXED the crack in the floor? How hard would it have been to repair it, or at least toss a goddamn low-pile rug over it? Was *low-pile* a real word? Vara thought of when Madame Bradshaw had said in front of the entire French class that she couldn't understand why Vara wasn't better at languages. "I mean, considering your *heritage*." All the other kids looked at Vara, who enlisted every muscle in the effort not to cry. At the bell she ran to the girls' bathroom, locked the stall, and let the tears come. She had spent her childhood seeing whites look at her a beat too long, hearing them ask where she was from "originally" and did she speak her "own" language. Forehead pressed to the stall door, she stared at new gray scuffs on the sneakers she had washed the day before and made a vow: she would speak English better than any white person, including her father—descendant of Mayflower riders, Korean War veteran, real estate agent, asshole. Language would be her knife. "I'm done, can I be excused?" "A standing rib roast is done," her father said, "but a young lady is finished." "I'm finished, can I be excused?" He waited, staring; Vara had made an error; but what was it? I'm finished, I have finished, can I be, could I be—"*May* I be excused?" "You may." "Thank you," Vara said, aching in every gland for revenge.

Ant came into the Fish Bowl, biting an apple. "Hey there, Vera."

Her whole life, the misapprehension. Sorry, I thought it was Vee-ra. Unseen and too-seen. You're so tall for an Asian person!

"How's your day going?" Ant said.

"It's . . . going."

"I hear you. I've been staring at the computer so long my eyes are like potato chips."

"The dissertation?" They were writing about slavery and the British Gothic.

"Yeah, I'm finishing a chapter about this huge domed house William Beckford built, called Fonthill Abbey, which kept collapsing under its own weight, and Beckford was thought to be insane because he wouldn't stop building it, even though it was literally turning into ruins. His hubris and grandiosity echoed the racist colonial logic of the Jamaican sugar plantations, which were the source of his family's wealth."

"Didn't Beckford sometimes order dinner for twelve when he was eating by himself?"

"Yes!" Ant grabbed Vara's arm, which sent a thrill up her throat. "I love that you know this!"

"I read *Vathek* in college."

"And he named one of his dogs Viscount Fartleberry."

"The things people do," Vara said, instantly regretting it: the phrase made her sound so bland.

Ant nodded. "People do a lot of things."

Why had Vara shut down the conversation with that phrase? *I am not bland!* she wanted to cry. She longed to talk more about books with Ant, who was not just the only other person of color at the House but the only person equipped for a literary conversation. Caz didn't read; Lasko read vampire romances; Mrs. Quimbee had a book-clubbish like-or-dislike mentality. Marika may have been a reader, but she said so little about herself, Vara couldn't be sure.

At the first-floor elevator, she hit the UP button. Low slurp of the elevator doors. She rolled out on the second floor, where she almost hit Davey.

"Hello, Harold," Vara said.

"What'd you call me?" There were pom-poms on his head.

"Nothing," she said, rolling on toward her room.

Sunroom

HARP MUSIC ON THE SPEAKERS. Pastor Jeff in a white velour tracksuit. "Put the moon in your hands and follow it through the room." The pastor demonstrated holding the moon; Rudd laughed; Kestrel told him to be quiet.

"Splash down into the waves like a dolphin and rise up like a star."

Harp gave way to restaurant jazz.

"Catch flies with your spider fingers. Play the floating drum. You're a cavewoman gathering shrubs, gather gather."

"Nope," Rudd said. "That's me out." He aimed his walker at the door and made a sluggish beeline.

"Mr. Rudd," the pastor called, "would you rather be an otter holding hands with another otter, floating on your back?"

"Bollocks," Rudd yelled, continuing his departure.

"You are wavy, buzzy, fluid, heavy, floaty, tight, expansive. Surprise yourself by not knowing what your next move will be."

After fifteen minutes, Pastor Jeff turned off the music and lit a fat balsam candle. "Thank you, everyone, for being open to joy! Before we leave today, I'd like to say a few words about interconnection. About the tiny and not so tiny threads that link all beings to all other beings. We imagine ourselves as these totally separate entities, but is this accurate? Water to cloud to rain to earth to seed to plant to human body. I am the ocean, and the ocean is me. Think of a match. Until a human hand strikes it on a frictive plane, fire will not manifest. We can't comprehend the match apart from the hand striking it. Nor can we comprehend it apart from the flame that is always present within the match, waiting to appear."

Davey said, "*My* flame is definitely waiting to appear."

"Are you all aware," the pastor said, pacing the sunroom, "that emotional subvariants can vanish forever from the human population due to lack of use? For example, the sour-beige flavor of loneliness you feel when nobody's answering and you can't remember anyone else's number—that's almost extinct, thanks to cell phones. Extinct!"

"So true," Kestrel said.

"I'm too young to be acquainted with that sour-beige flavor," the pastor said, "but members of my congregation have told me about it in moving detail." He gave them a stupendous blue-eyed smile.

Office

CAZ STARED OUT the window, sucking on a licorice stick. Salt the walk and parking area, check. Buckets of sand on front and back steps, check. She only liked snow when she wasn't the one who had to deal with it. And this was only the beginning of the season. Down in town they were wild for Christmas, it was all inflatable reindeer and free eggnog at the fire station; but the holidays were hard at the House. The air got clammy with thoughts of dead people or of living people who weren't going to visit. Last year the persimmon pudding had tasted like matches. Everyone ate it anyway, politely.

"Knock, knock?" came a voice she couldn't place.

"Yeah?"

It was Pastor Jeff in his baffling tracksuit. "Hi there, neighbor!"

"How was Nia?"

"Oh, it was fun," he said. "Always among the highlights of my week."

There should be public teeth-whitening booths, Caz thought. Like charging stations for electric cars. Then everyone's teeth could gleam like Pastor Jeff's.

"I think of teaching," he added, "as a practice of being welcomed. When I work with someone's body, I am a *guest* of that body. And it's gratifying to see the hosts flourish. Mrs. Quimbee, for instance, is really starting to get her boogie on."

"Is she, now." He was a tool, but Caz would take all the community service she could get—exercise classes, gutter cleaning, secondhand rugs for the cold floors. And cash: he'd bought the back acre last spring at the first price she quoted. He'd mentioned wanting to expand. Facing three years' worth of property taxes and late fines, she hadn't asked him to elaborate.

"Also." The pastor folded his arms across his chest. "Not sure if you're aware, but they're talking on the news about two missing children."

"Yeah, I got an amber alert." Chest fluttering, forehead taut.

"A girl and a boy who ran away from foster care."

"I hope they're okay."

He smiled. "I think you've done more than hope."

"What?"

"Whoever welcomes this little child in my name welcomes me, and whoever welcomes me welcomes the one who sent me. For it is the one who is least among you all who is the greatest."

"Sorry?"

"Marika's great-granddaughter bears a striking resemblance to the photo on the news," he said.

She rolled her shoulders back, which usually made her feel more capable. "Look, we haven't—"

"I know they're here, Caz. But no judgment!" He raised his palms. "I applaud you for opening your door."

"I'm going to drive them back to Child Protective Services as soon as the roads are clear."

"Have you notified CPS?"

"Not yet. There's been a lot going on. But we will."

"I have no doubt." The smile turned into a rapt, shining frown. "Listen, those kids must have really hated being in care, if they went to such lengths to escape. Sounds as if they haven't found the right family yet. A loving, stable home where they can thrive. Two of my own children are adopted, you know."

"Yep, you've mentioned that."

"And a lot of folks in my congregation are involved in fostering. They're all great people, so much love to give, such a beautiful way to answer the call to service. I think—"

"Hello? Anybody in there? Hello?" Rudd thudded in on his walker, scowling.

"You've got a flock to tend," the pastor told Caz. "But let's circle back to this, yeah?" He winked at her. "Mr. Rudd! How's the shoulder?"

"Nobbut middlin," he said.

"Patience, friend. Healing will come."

When Pastor Jeff was gone, Rudd raised one finger in Caz's direction. "I'm here to warn you."

"Uh-oh."

"About one of the youngsters. He's been putting his own nail clippings into the night snack and I'm strugglin to work out the reason why. The nails get all mixed in with the custard, which I will never touch again. Good thing I'm no stranger to starving."

"That guy no longer lives here." What had Sparkle Tooth meant by "circle back"?

"Oh, well done! You also want to keep an eye on the lad all covered in spiders. I'm not sure we can trust him."

"That's Davey. Would it help if everyone wore name tags?"

Rudd sniffed. "Help is a strong word. I will see you at Community Meeting."

Fish Bowl

THERE WAS ENOUGH light to see each other's faces by, but not enough to feel entirely seen, especially for those in the corners, at the grainy perimeter, where the light started to stop. The sounds from their bodies competed with the heat from the overhead bulb caged in pale plastic and the green table lamp and the red lamp on the rolltop desk that reminded Rudd of his daughter's apartment and the rest of them of nothing at all.

Lasko had stacked wood and newspaper in the fireplace. Caz looked at the kindling without the energy to find a match for it, and calculated that if she'd had a kid at seventeen and the kid had a kid at eighteen, then Davey could be her grandson. Marika pictured Rudd's face hitting the floor after she tripped him. Rudd wished Georgie would visit. Mrs. Quimbee counted the days until her grandchildren would visit. Kestrel counted the persons she had slept with, in chronological order. Fronzi wondered when food. Vara wondered how many hours it took a human body to freeze to death. Ant thought about how to weave Barthes's idea of the Neutral into their current chapter. Davey thought what if you got crosshairs tattooed on your eyeballs so that everyone you saw would be in your sights.

Ringing a small bronze bell: "Let's go around and do names and pronouns. I'm Caz. She/her."

"Prick a doodle doo, the pronouns again?"

"We have some newer residents," she told Rudd, "so it helps to revisit, especially—"

"My name is Mr. Rudd. I'm a man."

When they got to Davey, chin on jeaned knee in the corner, he said, "I'm a soldier, so my pronoun is 'soldier' or 'specialist.'"

"Those obviously aren't pronouns," Vara said.

"Maybe they are now," he said.

"Let's open it up to community contributions."

Kestrel, shelling pistachios at the piano: "The kids who came to sing the other day? Can that please definitely never happen again?" Pale green dust all over the keys.

"I thought they were very cute," Mrs. Quimbee said.

"I saw one of the little fuckers kick Frenzy," Davey said.

"Fronzi."

The dog raised her head, then lowered it to nuzzle Vara's socked foot.

"Whatever, it got kicked."

"The whole situation," Kestrel said, "was problematic."

"Problematic how? They were middle schoolers."

"They called me Frankenstein!" Rudd said.

"Which, yes, was not cool," Caz said. "But—"

"Isn't Community Meeting a time to air grievances?"

"Valid grievances."

Kestrel licked her fingertips. "Valid according to who?"

"Pipe *down*," Rudd said. "Let her run the meeting."

"Hard pass," Kestrel said.

"You're a tiresome girl. No door on your mouth."

"Oh really? Then let's talk about the rubber donut you're sitting on. Does it give your hemorrhoids enough room to stretch out?"

"Piss off," Rudd said. She deserved a taste of her own medicine. Always pointing out how the rest of them weren't up to snuff. Whose daughter was she? Was her dad getting a little money sent every month by her? His own girl used to tuck a few dollars into her letters, but no longer.

Vara farted softly.

Smelling it, Adeline declared: "Barking spider."

"Anyway, *next*," Caz said, "I want to mention that James and Nola will be leaving tomorrow, once the roads are plowed."

The cold logs were quiet under the chimney. Fronzi yawned.

"Where will they go?" Marika said.

"They'll be—with James's mom."

"Back in their own beds," Mrs. Quimbee said, nodding.

"Where's the father?" Rudd said.

"Not part of their lives, evidently."

"I can't imagine," Rudd said.

"Why can't you imagine?" Marika snapped. "Is it such an uncommon story?" To Caz she said, "Bring the boy's mother here. They can all three live with us."

"In a perfect world."

"Why not in this world? I'll pay for the kids' expenses, and his mother can do chores like the other youngs, and it won't be any extra burden."

A pressed green silence.

"I am not joking," Marika said.

"I know," Caz said.

"Or we could apply to be their foster family."

"That would take months," Vara murmured.

The silence lay over them, greener, until Caz said briskly, "We'll say our goodbyes tomorrow. And—this is important—we're not going to tell anyone they were here."

"Who would we tell?" Mrs. Quimbee said. "The mailman? I never even see the mailman."

"The parents of your grandchildren."

Quimbee shrugged. "I'm not a snitch."

Davey stood up. "Is this over yet?"

"Not quite," Caz said. The smell of his aftershave as he brushed past, on his way into the hall, sparked a quick throb in her pussy. "I need to alert everyone to a change in the common-space guidelines. As of next week, television hours in the Fish Bowl will begin at six p.m."

"Wait, what?"

"Almost sounded like you said six *pee*-em."

"Which I did."

"No!"

"But my show starts at two!"

"This is cruel."

"How can I watch my show?"

"Have you ever heard," Kestrel said, "of an amazing invention called the internet? You can watch a lot of shows there. Some might even say *every* show."

"Have you ever heard of 'I don't have a computer'?"

More cries of outrage. Adeline threw her stuffed fox at Caz's head, but missed.

"To encourage us all to *connect!*" Caz said. "Talk to each other! Instead of just staring at—"

"Bollocks."

"Nah."

Caz retrieved Bunty the fox from the corner and dropped him into Adeline's lap. "Loneliness," she said, "kills more people every year than smoking does." Was this statistic even true? "All right. That's it. Snack tonight is lemon bars," she added, and a few people cheered.

As the room slackened, Ant leaned toward Caz and said, "Can I talk to you for a minute?"

Sunroom

"FIRST THING I WANT TO SAY is that I believe in what the House is trying to do. Your vision for it. I think intergenerational collective living is an ethical formation, much more so than the nuclear family. It's like Graeber said: 'the ultimate, hidden truth of the world is that it is something we make, and could just as easily make differently.' Which is why I wanted to live here. I mean, that and the free rent."

Ant smiled, but Caz didn't smile back. She was in a mood, apparently. Or maybe her defensiveness was kicking up. Maybe she was expecting Ant to say something critical—which, of course, Ant could, starting with how about paying the Black woman you employ a better hourly wage? (Polly hadn't minded sharing how much she made as an aide.) Not the time for that. "And it's cool that James and Nola are here. Honestly they should stay as long as they want. But Caz? You need to be a little more worried about the cops."

"I'm not *not* worried," she said, in such a hoarse voice that Ant changed their mind: it wasn't moodiness or wariness so much as flat-out exhaustion.

"Well, what's your plan if they show up? I got an amber alert. They aren't playing."

"Kids'll be gone tomorrow."

"But if somebody comes by tonight?"

"No one's coming in weather like this."

Exhaustion, plus whiteness.

Kitchen

JAMES WALKED ON HIS TIPTOES to the porch door, which had a window he wasn't tall enough to see out of. He tried the doorknob: no. He liked being in the kitchen—the warm colors, the smooth hard patches of floor—but he didn't want to be in here for as long as Nola and Lasko did. They seemed content to sit forever at the wooden table, drinking tea that smelled crinkly. James had his own water bottle at the House, a brick red one, which he took now from the counter and turned upside down and rattled against the butcher block until he saw the spraying drops.

"Bear, stop!"

He grinned at Nola, still rattling.

"Oh my God," but she wasn't mad. She got up and grabbed the bottle. "I'm taking this away until you can stop spilling." To Lasko she said, "Do you have a towel?"

"Don't worry," he said, "it's only a little bit, I'll deal, but—communitymeetingjustended and I need togetnightsnackready, so—?"

To James's relief, Nola beckoned him to follow her out of the kitchen.

Fish Bowl

LASKO CAME IN carrying a giant aluminum tray. "Welcome to No-*vemm*-ber," he sang, "when everyone's seasonal affective disorder starts to kick in."

"That is not a medical diagnosis, you know," Marika said.

"Actually—"

"Artery plaque is a medical diagnosis. Moping is not. Splash some cold water on your face."

"Wow, love the gaslighting!" Lasko said. "And the denial of the body-mind connection."

"My dear deluded periwinkle," Mrs. Quimbee said, inspecting the tray with her napkin at the ready.

Night snack was the best idea Nola had heard of in a long time. Dinner didn't have to be the end; you were guaranteed more food a few hours later. She couldn't believe it happened every single night. The tray came out at eight p.m. sharp. Tonight it was glistening yellow squares dusted with flat sugar.

"Lemon bars, thank Christ. Remember what I told you, girl: avoid the custard."

Mrs. Quimbee said that Rudd suffered from paranoid fantasies and Nola could eat as much custard as she wanted, but the lemon bars were excellent, too.

A show about undercover narcotics detectives in the Outer Hebrides had begun. Nola sat on the green couch, next to Ms. Dragon, with a second bar on a napkin on her knee. She noticed a spider on Ms. Dragon's face, small and brown at the temple where the hair stopped. Did she not wash herself? Brown ones could be deadly. The spider's leg caught in a wrinkle, then yanked free, kept going, up into the dark-gray hair, a thick mess loosely gathered and pinned. Somebody should give her a bath. But there weren't many staff people. Not enough to rinse off spiders. Vara had referred to Ms. Dragon as a survivor, meaning, presumably, she was so tough she wouldn't mind bugs crawling on her? Maybe Nola had misheard—instead of *survivor* Vara had said *imbiber*— but would a drunk pay such careful attention to James's shoelace? Would a drunk hide the shoelace in the blue folds of her dress and wait patiently for him to find it?

"Not if you plan on getting out of Griminish alive!" the detective said.

"Do you want more tea? I can bring you some."

Marika looked at her. "You try to please everyone, don't you?"

Nola shrugged.

"I suppose," Marika said, "you've been trained as most girls are, to put other people's comfort first."

"That's not why." She hadn't been too pleasing in the psychiatrist's office, when he prescribed medication because she was acting out. You were supposed to act *in*. You were not supposed to start screaming and keep screaming until they allowed you and James to sleep in the same room. You were not supposed to hit the caseworker in the penis when he tied James to the bed.

"Then why?" Marika said.

She shrugged again.

Marika blew her nose twice, then pushed the tissue back under her sleeve cuff. She could guess that the reason for the niceness was to protect James. On the day she'd thrown scissors at the neighbor boy for mocking her brother, she had been pierced by a sensation more thrilling, more real, than any other she'd yet experienced. About Nola's age, she'd been. The blood and crying and whipping afterward hadn't mattered: that sensation was worth it.

You had to be loud, not nice.

You had to make noise, shake the bells, so the wolves would think twice.

Awkwardly patting Nola's thigh, she said, "You aren't alone, you know."

James went to stand in front of the screen.

"Move, please," Mrs. Quimbee whispered.

"James, move!" Nola shouted, and he gave her the side-eye, and Marika grinned to see the pleasure he was taking in the disruption. *May you take such pleasure your whole life long, mílo mou.*

"Does that little pistachio ever rest?" Mrs. Quimbee said. "If he would just *sit down*, maybe he could enjoy the program. How can he enjoy anything if he's always wandering around?"

"How can *you* enjoy anything if you're always yapping?" Rudd said.

"Cheeky mastodon," Mrs. Quimbee said.

It occurred to Marika—the fact emerging from some derelict crevice of her mind—that the word *mastodon* meant "breast-tooth." James came to lean against her knees. Pressed his hand into her forearm. The best feeling. She pulled him into a hug and whispered, "Did you know that Mr. Rudd is a cheeky breast-tooth?" and breathed in his wonderful soft little-boy smell.

He scratched her neck, hard.

She reached up and touched wetness.

"Oh my God I'm so sorry!" Nola said. "Are you okay? James, we *don't do that*. You hurt Ms. Dragon."

James laughed.

"Jesus, you're bleeding," Rudd said.

"I'm all right," Marika said. She took the tissue from her sleeve and patted her neck with it.

Nola clamped her hands onto James's shoulders. "Don't laugh, this isn't funny. You hurt her."

"He really ought to apologize," Mrs. Quimbee said.

"I am fine, goddammit!" Marika barked.

"Come on, bear. Let's take a break." She led James by the hand out of the Fish Bowl into the front hall, where he headed straight for the potted plants. She didn't care what he did to the plants. "Not one single fuck given," as Stell liked to say. At home they watched *The Golden Girls* after dinner and James, roaming, would pause once in a while to nuzzle Stell's neck or pinch Nola's arm or laugh when they tickled him. He'd known that when the episode ended it would be time for his bath. "Sluts just heal quicker," Sophia said, and Stell said, "That is so true!" and Nola wanted a patio exactly like theirs, outdoors but hidden from other people. In Florida its name was *lanai*. And Stell said, "You can never lose him. Look at me, Nola. *Never*."

Kitchen

IN 1944, AFRAID THE GERMANS would soon invade America, the sea captain had ordered his sons to build a bunker under the kitchen garden. They started with buckets and pickaxes, digging out a narrow tunnel from the scullery. The war ended before the bunker was ready. The tunnel became a storage closet, a hiding place.

LASKO LEANED AGAINST THE BUTCHER BLOCK, munching a radish and contemplating the white latticework on the wall. That goddamn latticework—he had always wondered what was behind it. It wasn't his place to investigate. Unless, actually, it was? His gaze moved around the room: kettle shining on the stove with its reechy burner wells, cups and plates stacked tight, dish towels bright on their nails. What was this kitchen, if not his place? Lasko's cooking and planning, his trips to town for groceries, kept the House alive.

A few minutes with a hammer and chisel was enough to pry up and pull off the painted metal panel. Behind it was a raw-walled chamber, a dank odor. Butter and cream and sawdust? Squatting with the flashlight, Lasko got as close as he dared. No sign of rodents. He couldn't tell how far back the chamber went. There was a stray brick, shoved several feet inside—was it a brick? Or could it have been a money-box? A diary? Lasko stretched his arm in, praying that a hidden rat would not attack. The object was furred with dust, it felt like pressing his hand into a million dead moths, he drew it out slowly, breath held, eyes closed, then opened his eyes. It was, after all, only a brick.

But he could turn the brick into something else. For his novel.

Lasko was brainstorming a story set in a house very much like this one, in mountains very much like these. It would be a short, tense novel with thriller qualities but more melancholy. He needed to write the brick down so that it could become something else.

"Lasko?"

He closed his notebook and smiled. The children stood before him, neither of them looking especially happy.

"Do you mind if James has some saltines?"

He didn't mind. At least, he didn't think he did. He was so accustomed to staying alert to other people's emotions, responding to their needs, that sometimes he couldn't tell how he felt, or whether he was feeling at all. Another person, he reflected on his way to the pantry, might have minded tremendously if they got interrupted while they were working on their novel.

James took his crackers over to the sink and picked up the whisk Lasko had left for him in the drying rack.

"What were you writing?" Nola said.

"Oh, just—I'm not sure yet. Do you like to write?"

"Not really."

"Fair enough," Lasko said.

"Ghee-ah ghee-ah!" James said.

"You know the preacher who's your neighbor?"

"Pastor Jeff."

"Why was he here yesterday?"

"He asked if we wanted the boys from the teen fellowship to clean our gutters again this year." Lasko shook his head. "Caz says we should take every ounce of help that comes our way, but . . ."

"What was in the bag?"

"Zucchini muffins. His wife never stops baking. I said we couldn't accept them because of the walnuts. I said the gutters, yes, but we don't allow nuts on the premises due to food allergies."

"Which isn't true," Nola said, smiling.

"Which isn't true! Only peanuts are banned. But I can't stand that guy."

A cascade of high-pitched thuds, then spinning metal, then a wail—James had knocked several cans of Ensure off the counter. Lasko sensed Nola watching, waiting to see if James would get in trouble. He laughed and said, "Do you know how many calories are rolling around on that floor right now?"

James retreated to his spot by the butcher block, where he sat cross-legged, whisk in hand. Nola started picking up the cans.

If the police came, they could hide the kids in the soundproofed room. Neither of them ate that much. The grocery budget had been shrinking each month, in increments so tiny Caz probably thought Lasko wouldn't notice; so he'd started buying the generic of everything. He had been sleeping late yesterday morning when Davey appeared at his door with a cryptic message: "Some kids are on the back porch and Caz says come down." On the porch Lasko had found a duct-tape-covered backpack. Beside it, in a little heap, was a sheet with holes cut out of it: two for the arms, two for the eyes, one for the mouth.

He opened his notebook and wrote:

Possible Events
A ghost is up to shenanigans
Letters wrapped in oilcloth found in kitchen tunnel
"Hikers" (evil) come to the door
Murder in the village; someone at the house accused
Electricity cut off by human hands

What shenanigans would the ghost get up to? Who had written the letters? Would Lasko actually write this book? And if he did, would it ever get published? Painters in nineteenth-century France who'd been snubbed by the main art galleries could show their work at the Salon of the Refused. It was a home for rejects. The trash was the treasure.

"What I'm writing is a mystery novel," he told Nola, who had built a pyramid of Ensure cans on the counter.

Vara rolled in from the hall. "Lasko? Polly can't get here tonight, with all the snow. Could you do Adeline's bedtime?"

"We really need to hire another aide," he muttered.

"But for now—"

"Yeah. Yes. James, close the freaking refrigerator, please!"

Fish Bowl

MARIKA TOOK HER preferred spot at the fireplace end of the green couch, pulled out the wadded tissue, dabbed one nostril, and tucked the tissue back under the cuff. A minor-key police procedural set in Manchester had begun. She liked the murder shows because cops weren't good at feelings. Characters on soaps and sitcoms expressed themselves too easily. Where was the shame and aversion, the incoherent longing? In the opening minutes of any procedural, when the detectives ducked under yellow tape to reach a body, her own body relaxed. They asked the forensic pathologist for time of death; the pathologist couldn't say for sure; Marika's shoulders unclenched.

"These bite marks," the pathologist said.

"Dog?" the detective said.

"Guess again."

"Fox?"

"No, a wolf did this."

The scar-lipped detective frowned. "There haven't been wolves in England since the fifteenth century. Except for zoos."

"We've seen this episode," Mrs. Quimbee announced. "The grief-stricken professor was seeking vengeance for—"

"Stop talking!" Marika said.

Quimbee had been known to hijack the clicker, which Marika now guarded in the folds of her blue dress. Watching TV was not a democracy. She pressed the volume up. Wolves had been plentiful once in the forests and mountains of Greece, hated by shepherds, cursed by farmers, feared by all. Whoever fed the wolf in the winter, they said, would be eaten by him in the spring.

At the commercial Marika looked over at Kestrel, who was tapping on her phone.

"Social media," Kestrel explained, though Marika hadn't said anything. "You know what that is, right? Randos judging a ruthless curation of your shadow self?"

"Sounds very special," Marika said. She knew what social goddamn media was. What did Kestrel take her for?

"I love it. Otherwise, all the way out here, life would feel, I don't know—small."

"Small? So what. Give me strong black tea and a murder show, I'm happy."

"Or if not happy, then content."

"I said happy."

"But not, like, deliriously."

"Why should anyone be deliriously happy?"

Still typing, Kestrel laughed. "Why shouldn't we?"

"That's the greedy wish of a child. You know, my sister had a mole like yours, except hers had two hairs, not three."

"Wow, that really." *Tap tap tappety tap.* "Makes me." *Tappety tap tap tap.* "Feel good. By the way I intentionally don't." *Tap, tap.* "Remove my facial hair, for obvious reasons."

Which were? wondered Marika. "I understand English quite well. You can speak at a regular pace."

"This is just, like, how I talk."

"Could you change how you talk?"

Kestrel pushed herself up into sitting position. "Fuck you, Ms. Dragon."

"Fuck you, too."

Kestrel's name she remembered because *sharp* gave her *falcon*. This sharp, soft, abundant girl would not have felt insulted by the mole remark if she knew what Marika's sister had looked like. Marika used to taunt her sister with a line from Aeschylus:

"Destroyer of ships, destroyer of men, destroyer of cities!" and Irini would say, "I'd rather be beautiful than Greek," but she had been both—she and Theo the beauties, Marika and Perna the plains. Their mother told Marika, "Irini won't have her beauty for long, and you, my apple, will have your brain forever." Helen of Troy. Irini of Salonika. Marika of the House, where she could see the river from her room.

Kestrel would come to appreciate, one day, what she'd had here. Breakfast seven to eight. Lunch eleven-thirty. Dinner five-fifteen. Night snack eight p.m. and watch the murder shows. A life as good as any other.

"*Why* must he use so much cardamom?" Mrs. Quimbee said. "This is inedible."

"And yet you are eating it."

"Cardamom is an aphrodisiac," Kestrel said.

Mrs. Quimbee scraped the last dollop from the ramekin. "You're thinking of nutmeg."

"No I'm pretty sure it's—"

"The other day my granddaughter said the smartest thing about muffins. Called them 'baby cakes.'"

"Is that smart?" Marika said.

Mrs. Quimbee's mouth stiffened. "She's three."

"I don't find it impressive, even for three." She wasn't going to lie just to keep a mouth from looking like that.

"Can I give you a piece of advice?"

"You may." Marika fingered the hidden clicker.

"You probably want to purchase a stronger deodorant?"

"Oh shit," Kestrel murmured.

"I'm sorry to be blunt," Mrs. Quimbee said, "but lately you've been smelling like—"

"Insomnia?" Marika said. "Do I smell like insomnia?"

"That wasn't—"

"Do you find my insomniac odor *foul*?"

"My goodness, if you'd let me get a word in."

If Quimbee had been able to get a word in, what she would've loved to say, Marika imagined, what she longed deep down to say, was: *You smell like a Jew.*

Marika rose and walked out of the Fish Bowl, billows swishing, clicker in hand. If Quim ever provoked her past tolerating, she would tell her what the word *quim* meant.

She stood in the hall listening for the boy who reminded her so much of her brother.

Where was he? What room?

She heard nothing as she climbed the stairs.

It was obvious that the murdering wolf would end up being a man.

Some people had carnivorous faces, eyes set close together, the better to see prey with, while other faces were more herbivorous, one eye over to each side because plant eaters didn't need a straight-ahead gaze.

The lichen *Letharia vulpina* contained vulpinic acid, fatal to carnivores. People in the far north used to hide this lichen inside dead reindeer, sometimes accompanied by broken glass, as a way to kill wolves.

Marika's grandmother had come from mountains where they once protected their goats by making noise. Hand-cast brass bells were tied by suspension loops to leather collars. The strongest and fastest villagers had worn the collars around their necks or held them like tambourines and followed the herd, dancing and shaking, a roaming wall of sound. Wolf bells. The purpose was to draw the wolves toward you and away from the sick, slow, old, or very young stragglers who would have been, without this interference, easily picked off. Being chosen to wear the bells had been an honor, because it took courage: you weren't safe from wolf attacks, merely better equipped to fend them off. Unlike an injured goat lagging after the others, the humans had rifles and leather greaves and skill. Marika's grandmother had worn the bells well into her first pregnancy. Wolf bells protected *all* members of a herd, even those who couldn't run, even those who were close to death—they could die in comfort, not drenched with terror in the jaws of a beast.

Screw Darwin, Marika thought.

Fish Bowl

"MY GHOUL," KESTREL voice-to-texted, "I miss you a lot. There's a bunch of snow here. I helped Lasko bake gingerbread for Frankenstein, and we talked about our horrible families. I told him about prettiest one / best one. When Lasko got an abortion in college his mom found out and said she would never forgive him for, quote, doing away with, unquote, her grandchild. Families of origin are so gross."

If the House were a family, Vara would be the mother and Caz the aunt and Ms. Dragon the great-aunt and Lasko the uncle. Kestrel would be the lust-sick daughter who pined for the local bartender. The only un-hot thing about the bartender was her breath. If Kestrel started fucking the bartender, she would use mouthwash for the both of them. She would shoot her minty breath down her throat and taste the cleanness of her own tongue. Tongues weren't even that great—lips were so much hotter, their wet softness, the ways they searched. Kissing was strange in that there was no ultimate arrival. You just tried and tried and tried to get somewhere. But where were you trying to get? All the way into the person's mouth? Down their throat? When Kestrel wanted someone, she had the urge to swallow them whole.

Her mother had told her that if two people stayed together long enough, they stopped kissing. A peck hello or goodnight, yes, but you didn't *make out* anymore. This was too heinous to be true. Even if her mother had stopped kissing her first husband, then stopped kissing Kestrel's father, then stopped kissing Kestrel's stepfather, it didn't mean *everyone* stopped. Her mother would have qualified for a diagnosis of delusional narcissist, though she had never darkened a psychologist's door. Kestrel once heard her say, when she thought she was alone: "I'm not the prettiest one, but I'm the *best* one."

Things hadn't reached the agony stage with the bartender yet—the part where the fact of her not loving Kestrel became unbearable. The agony stage was Kestrel's favorite, because you were more alive, then, than you were during most of your life. Just *existing*, staying upright, was most of your life; but once in a while you had the little strips of fire under your fingernails and the chemicals pulsing in your chest, the beating of wings against your ribs from the fact of this other body on Earth with you, the sheer luck of having been born in the same lifetime: and this, the luck, could always be hers, even if the bartender didn't love her back. Those thighs swelling under those bedazzled jeans were on Earth with Kestrel, and so was the paradox of the bad breath, and so was the fact that when the bartender said "Hey, Miss K" a hot arrow pushed through her lungs and into her belly down to her clit.

From Mrs. Quimbee came a tinkling snore; Kestrel kicked her slipper and she jerked awake. Caz, from the doorway: "Will you make sure to turn off the lamps before you go up?"

The Fish Bowl windows didn't have curtains and the black night pressed close, one branch tapping the glass like it wanted to come in. Get ahold of yourself, Miss K. Stop being afraid of a tree. Stop picturing the grinning face of the killer who can see you right now and who is calculating how long it will take to starve you in a hole in his basement before your skin gets loose enough for him to wear.

Davey's Room

HIS MOUTH WAS open a little, and Caz could see the chipped front tooth. He lay on his side, one arm squashed by his ribs, the other bent above his heart, fist lodged at his chin. He had bad dreams only, he'd told her, the same terrible few repeating for years. Steamrollers crushing yellow flowers on the granite surface of the moon. A sea of mouths making noises like televisions. His breath was loud and steady enough to mean he wouldn't feel Caz drifting there, reaching for but not quite touching the hard curve of muscle above his elbow. If she were to touch it, would he mutter *What* or would he grab her and pull her down?

But when he started to wake up, she didn't want him to be awake.

He was getting hard—engorged stem batting against her belly.

"Say it."

"Fuck me," she said.

"Again."

"Fuck me."

He pinned her hands behind her head. A shudder of pain moved across his face. He let go of her hands and rolled away, gasping, "Sorry."

"Is it the reflux?"

"Yeah," he said. "Motherfucking *shit*."

"Can you take some of the—"

"Vara doesn't have any more."

"Then you need to call the doctor, or get some over-the-counter."

"I don't like the doctor," Davey said.

"Ask for a different one."

"I mean, *the doctor*. As in, all of them." He dropped his fore-head to his elbow, his face dark red, the cheekbones jumping forward.

Caz wanted to leave.

She wanted to be in her own room, her own quiet.

"Did you ever almost die?" he said.

"Maybe," she said.

"From trying to kill yourself?"

"No, not that."

"Not *ever*?"

"Not intentionally."

Davey twisted Caz's nipple between his thumb and forefinger. Leaned to lick it. "I think we should have sex in my car."

She laughed. "Right now?"

"I mean, at some point. I never fucked in a car but I predict it would be cool."

"It's overrated," Caz said. She pictured the mud-green uphol-stery of the back seat he used to sleep on.

"Is it true you were famous?"

"Um—kind of. But the kind where you don't get rich. We had one big record. Big as in people with good taste liked it, not as in sold a million copies. Our drummer could be kind of a dick, and he and Vara hated each other. Once Vee got so mad at him she was crying and yelling that she'd pull out every semen-drenched hair on his head, and West goes, 'My wig is strong,' all casual."

"That was a random story. Where is he now?"

"Dead."

"Oh." His hand stopped on her knee. "I have a good band name idea."

"Thrill me."

"Anal Dining."

"Hand me a cigarette?"

Springing off the bed to get the pack, Davey scooped up something else from the chair. "Check out this fucked-up hat my mom sent."

"Are those *pom*-poms?"

"Yeah, because she's corny." He took off the hat, but kept holding it.

IF THEY HAD NOT BEEN ASSIGNED to the same seventh-grade French class. If a guy in Caz's apartment building had not been selling his Candy Apple Red Stratocaster. If Vara had not dropped out of college. The tiny serendipities.

Vara had searched for role models: musicians who weren't boys and weren't white. She found Poly Styrene, Alice Bag, Annabella Lwin, and Vulpess. When Caz showed up to a soundcheck in dayglo-orange tights, Vara wouldn't play until she took them off. *Poly's mine. You can't have her.* Caz had dismissed this reaction as melodramatic. So much, back then, she'd been quick to dismiss. She hadn't given Vara an inch of compassion for getting married and quitting the band to move a thousand miles away with her shiny-lipped husband. She understood Vara better now, decades too late.

> Wrecked ship, I have a crush on your cargo crates
> and on the monster in those cargo crates
> and on the taste of that iceberg
> if I could get it into my mouth.

Years after Bolts had broken up, twelve seconds of "Freezing Summer" was used in a commercial promoting tourism to Iceland, and fans still bothered to denounce Caz for it online. What had happened to the grimy freak they loved? Their screeching goddess would never have stooped to a commercial. She had felt basically fine about stooping. After rehab and the halfway house, she had zero money.

The marketing team, who had picked the song for its beat, muted the vocal track. Nobody wanted a tourism commercial about getting it into my mouth. The song described what had happened after the Mount Tambora volcano erupted in 1815, when volcanic ash spread, on the wind, around the world. In most of the northern hemisphere, temperatures had dropped and the sun disappeared. They called 1816 the year without a summer. It snowed in July. Crops couldn't grow. There was no bread, or the bread was criminally expensive. A quart of wheat for a day's wages, as the Bible once promised. Hunger rode in on black horses slick with lava. The starving became refugees, thousands and thousands crossing borders of countries, whole oceans; and lots of them got sick. Scared of disease, the wealthy barred the refugees from their towns. People ate grass and licked crumbs and thought about drowning their kids in the Rhine. The same year, in a villa in Switzerland, not starving, Mary Shelley wrote the first pages of *Frankenstein*. Thus strangely are our souls constructed.

First you saw a volcano, then a glacier, then a remote mountain road above whose curves the camera calmly glided. Then the drums surged in, fast and heavy, irresistible, and the camera sped up. Glittery throbs of guitar. The last shot was of a giggling couple in the steamy turquoise water of a hot spring. "Iceland," said a rugged voice. "Otherworldly, but close to home."

When the commercial aired, Caz was working at a vintage store and fucking a potter. Her stomach hurt most of the time. She quit coffee, ate yogurt and kimchi, didn't want to see a doctor because they were all such assholes. The pain and bloating got so bad that the owner of the vintage store, who was also her ex-boyfriend, threatened to fire her unless she dealt with it. Turned out there was a jungle inside her. A tumor was choking one ovary; her uterus was a bloody balloon. They would need to take everything out, said the surgeon, *the whole shebang*, in a procedure known as debulking. The surgeon wanted to know if Caz had someone to help her process the grief of losing her ability to procreate. She wanted to stay on his good side, because he was going to cut her open, so she said "Sure" instead of "Douchebag, I'm forty-six and I've had three abortions." Her disinterest in reproducing hadn't wavered since high school, yet people would smile knowingly and say she would come to regret it. Even the potter, a man who rejected most American social norms, such as paying taxes, assumed she pined for a baby. He told her once she was welcome to use his sperm for a last-ditch attempt, as long as he bore no legal, financial, or emotional responsibility for the results.

The surgeon removed Caz's uterus and ovaries and Fallopian tubes, and scraped a few barnacles off her large intestine. On the hospital morphine she felt content, except when she remembered to be worried about losing her sex drive. She knew nothing, yet, about hormone therapies. Her foggy brain was crowded instead with information she didn't need—the year of Mount Tambora's eruption, the pick gauge she'd once preferred, the fact that she had been the only girl in tenth grade who couldn't make herself throw up.

The nurse asked if she liked ice cream.

"I want a necklace made of vitamins," she answered.

She was getting discharged that afternoon, would start chemo once her body was stronger. Which friend or family member would be coming for her? No, she couldn't just get a cab. Hospital policy. She had to have someone physically with her.

"What if a person doesn't have friends or family?"

"Is that your situation?"

"Well, it must be for some people," she said. "How do they get discharged?"

"A social worker takes them home." His face wore a look Caz

interpreted as I should probably ask this woman a compassionate follow-up question but I'm tired and my shift is about to end.

"Does it bother you when people refer to you as a male nurse?"

"Yes," he said, "although if I'm ranking the things that bother me, that wouldn't make the top ten."

The potter was free to leave his little wheel whenever he wanted, and thus had no excuse for not coming to pick her up, but he made one anyway: hospitals "upset" him.

"Have you ever met one single person who *likes* hospitals?" Caz yelled toward the phone receiver, which had slipped off her shoulder and was lodged between the plastic bed rail and her left breast.

"Burr-bah-burr-bah-burr-bah-burr," said the potter.

Her revenge would be to keep the pink-and-charcoal Fair Isle sweater he'd left at her apartment. She would miss his body and the scrumptious force it exerted on hers, but after the incisions healed and the chemo was done, she would find someone else to fuck. Assuming her sex drive survived the debulking. But why shouldn't it? What did Fallopian tubes have to do with arousal? She pushed the red button and when a nurse showed up she said, "The pain is really bad right now?" It was strategic to mention pain uncertainly while frowning slightly, rather than ask outright for morphine. (She had decided to put sobriety on hold while in the hospital.)

The only other number she could remember was Vara's parents', which she'd called hundreds if not thousands of times between the ages of twelve and seventeen. She expected Vara's mother to pick up the phone, but the person who answered was Vara herself. Her mother had just died, and she was there to clear out the house.

Caz hadn't spoken to her, at that point, in years. Lawyers had handled the Iceland commercial.

Ula's Room

THE SEA CAPTAIN'S DAUGHTER had lived at the top of the House when it was converted temporarily into a home for wounded soldiers. She was a widow with a child, but she giggled like a corked schoolgirl around a sergeant who didn't behave any better, despite the wife waiting for him in Texas. Ula fed him licorice from her own hand. One more, darlin, just one more. The village had recently built a mechanized lift to connect the main street with the houses on the cliff, and Ula and the sergeant rode the elevator together, kissing, until he went back to Texas and she went to cry in her room under the eaves.

Nola stood in this room hating the fact that it was morning again and she had to put on the same baggy light-blue jeans and ugly sweater and hideous shoes.

Enola Gay, you should have stayed at home yesterday.

Had Nola's mother ever stopped to consider how it would feel to be named after the plane that dropped an atomic bomb on Hiroshima? "It wasn't the *plane* you were named after, it was a song *about* the plane," as if that made a huge difference.

Enola Gay / Is mother proud of little boy today?

Nola wanted a name that hadn't killed hundreds of thousands of people.

She wanted her mother to not be in a correctional facility seventy-two miles away and her father not to be a saltine-colored man who had last been spotted at her eighth birthday party. (He'd brought a pack of puffy stickers; looked shy; left early.)

She wanted non-hideous shoes.

To want and not to have was a hardness across her—a shell. She was a hermit crab with the wanting all over her while the having floated beyond, beckoning, in sunlit water. She could have been content with not having if she didn't want, but she did want. Even if you couldn't control feelings, you could control (to quote her therapist) what you did with them. You could decide either to dance with a feeling or to bow and take your leave. The therapist had had several of these sayings and she would sit with her feet on a turquoise ottoman listening to them, not laughing, even though the sayings were so stupid she could have laughed. She could have made him, this socks-and-sandals therapist who had watered his office plants during their sessions, understand that she was not impressed. She'd hidden her scorn because she wanted him to help her and he wasn't going to help her if he didn't like her. The forbearance had gone wasted. Learning to be more assertive during phone calls with her mother had not been worth it. He couldn't help her with the main problem, which was wanting a life she didn't have.

Dining Room

"HOW CAN YOU STAND those without milk?" Mrs. Quimbee pointed at the bowl of dry O's Marika was eating with her fingers.

"I've stood worse."

"Oh aye?" Rudd said. "I grew up half-starved from rationing. They kept the rations going years after the war. I stole cream crackers from the teacher's desk and was never caught."

Marika cocked her head, staring at his mouth. "And were there no dentists in your war-torn country?"

"Save it."

"Did the cleaning and straightening of teeth—"

"More coffee?"

"—Violate local custom?" She nodded but did not push her mug toward Mrs. Quimbee, who had to reach for it. Where were the damn sugars? Marika squinted around. Across the table, Ant was eating toast and jabbing at their phone.

"Do you know where are the sugars?"

Ant looked up. "Want me to go check in the kitchen?"

"No, no, thank you, no." She wouldn't be seen wanting sugars. The tea cooled. Marika drifted.

"In Chicago," Ant was saying. "Then I went to college in Ohio."

Marika blinked. Whose question was this an answer to?

"And after graduation I moved to Flatbush."

"What is Flatbush?"

"A part of Brooklyn."

"The visual is disturbing," Marika said. "A hairy mons pubis pressed vertical—"

"Girl."

"Or woman."

Ant laughed. "No, I meant, like, *stop*."

They thought Marika had never set foot in Brooklyn. When they looked at her, they must have seen only death galloping fast. No future, no past. At seventeen years old, her stockings stiff with blood, Marika had walked off a ship onto Brooklyn, the first America she ever touched. Smelled of tar and sewage and gasoline. She'd allowed herself to remember her family only in the morning. Afternoons, she had mantras: "Bread, bread, bread, forget them!" Stole slices from loaves. Honed thief skills. "Apples, apples, apples, forget them!" Forgetting could be practiced. The sweetness of American apples had made her vomit. Before noon, in America, she allowed herself to think of Theo and his pinecone, Irini stitching a tablecloth for her marriage house, Perna belting out the "Hymn to Liberty" (voice like a donkey, but did that ever stop her?). Her sister with that honking voice had loved to sing. *I shall always know you by the dreadful sword you hold.* Whenever their father warned her to stop or he'd make her sorry, she had cranked her mouth wider. Loud, plain Perna. Loud, beautiful Theo. Eleven and nine when they were murdered by the Germans. Why had Marika lived instead? Such brawny joy her sister had taken in singing. She'd insisted on being loud. Why had Marika— less brave than Perna, less beautiful than Irini, less honest than Theo—been the one to stay alive?

Marika's Room

FROM A PLASTIC CONTAINER stowed with other plastic containers on the floor of her closet, she removed three gherkins. Rising from her knees, she groaned at a low-back spasm, though it was not the worst in her pain catalog, nowhere near. The pickles left a sour film in Marika's mouth. They were not artichokes, and she wanted them to be artichokes.

Artichoke with lemon, dill, and honey.

Like a long sound from the heaviest bell, her brother came over her. Theo, hold still. The dancing trees. Stop screeching. His fingers like birds on the pinecone. Too loud! She walked behind him and the trees danced and he watched. Wait, brother. Stop! Her heel hurt. Hot hill, red wind. Theo, screeching, grabbed a lemon from the dirt and bit.

She was his sister still, though he was dead, his sister always, she was the girl who walked behind him on a hill and she was the bag of spent muscle who hid the clicker in her dress. She was both girl and bag and neither and more, even when crushed into a single being by others. Here they called her Marika or Dragon or Ms. Dragon, shoving her into a name for a face shape. Her little brother hadn't called her anything; he was the only person in eighty-nine years who had never crushed her.

She was curious what the others here imagined she used to do or be, if they thought of her at all. She had more selves than they knew. Hearing that she once had been, by American standards, successful might have given Rudd a heart attack, so perhaps she would tell him.

Successful: she'd never seen a less interesting word. She had been that multiplication machine, but no longer, she lived minusly now, a wreck in the harbor with hair on her thighs. She went from room to room in her brain leaving pinecones at the doors, a prickly trail so that no one got lost—not brother, not sisters, not the soldiers who had killed them.

She lay on her bed to practice for the coffin. After the coffin she would turn into pure light and go straight down into the ocean. Her early people had painted eyes on the prows of their ships to make the ships see. The sailors had believed a shell of tree planks plowing tunnels through the black waves, its eyes mere crusts of chipped iris and peeling lash, could look ahead of itself. Greek ships drove waves so high the dolphins rode their walls. The dolphin was a savior of the shipwrecked and guider of souls to the underworld. Their hind legs had disappeared, in evolution, completely from view; a few bones remained, buried deep in their sides. A dolphin with an anchor symbolized—Marika forgot. But it symbolized something.

Easing herself off the bed, she went to the window, where the river was. Everyone here saw a different river—green, yellow, pewter-gray, slopping or shurring or flat as cloth—each brain knowing the word *river* through its own lacy contingencies, the form alone the same, an idea of riverness (place to catch trout; place to drown) that hardly resembled this particular river at all. Rivers were the thing to be crossed on the way, risking your horse fatally stumbling or the troll pulling you down with him under the bridge. There were tasks for the river: carry the logs to the mill near the port with a boat that would take the lumber to its future. Marika didn't know where this one went, or where it started, or what uses it had been put to over the centuries. It looked to her like a lead-colored ribbon.

She heard the clank of a toilet seat.

She heard the birds puttering on the roof. Her favorite one, puny-legged and footless, liked to huddle with her sister-birds in the mouth of the chimney.

Office

THE BELLS WERE RINGING from Church of the Lamb. Stell had said she would call at ten. Ten-oh-five, then ten-ten, and now ten-fifteen. Caz's phone was fully charged, the ringer on. She opened a new bag of black licorice and stared at the local news on her laptop. More snow was expected in the afternoon, so the plows hadn't gone out yet.

"Sorry," Stell said at ten-twenty. "It's been a morning. Still no luck with the car. James's father is a sack of shit. Are the kids okay?"

"They're fine, yeah. Are *you* okay?"

"Not really. But I will be, once I have the kids and we're settled. My sister is getting out in January, did I tell you? So she'll be with us again. That'll make a huge difference. It kind of sucks being the only grown-up, you know?"

"How long has she been in?"

"Three and a half years."

"We have two cars here," Caz said, before she knew she was going to say it.

"What?"

"One is the van, which we need for groceries and doctor's appointments and all that shit. The other one, though, you could take. It's an old Spectra, but it runs."

"Are you serious?"

Caz wasn't a mother (thank God) and she wasn't the greatest daughter. Sister, she could do. Lover. Comrade. The lateral kin.

"I'll drive the kids into town in the morning. They haven't plowed up here yet. You can meet us. Somewhere off the radar. Not your house, obviously."

"That would be—oh, Caz. You don't even know."

She would help Davey accept the sacrifice, convince him of its righteousness, once Stell and the kids were safely on their way.

Sunroom

SHORTLY BEFORE RUDD HAD COME to live at the House, he'd woken up in the ER on the other side of a plastic curtain from a nurse's station whose nurses were a talky bunch. "My testicle is weirdly so tender," one was saying when he came to. "Feels like it got *trampled* on."

"Trampled Sack Syndrome!" another said.

"Hi there, Mr. Rudd." Bearded, slender. "How we doing?"

"Hurts," Rudd said.

"Sorry to hear that."

"When can I leave?"

"Well, not immediately. You got pretty banged up."

"How?"

"In the accident."

Rudd had not been able to find any accident in his mind. He'd closed his eyes, trying. "Who hit me?"

"You drove your car into a fire hydrant. Your blood alcohol and tox screen were negative, so we're thinking you might have fallen asleep at the wheel. It happens. Especially when . . ."

"When what?"

"Lie back down, Mr. Rudd." The tender-balled nurse was typing on a wheelable computer. "Let's just be glad you came out of it with relatively minor injuries."

"You saying I'm too old to drive?"

"Sir, stop yelling."

But Rudd had not been. Yelling. He had not.

In the beeping half-dark, later—was it later?—he heard giggling.

"Test results are back for young Mr. Drunkybear! Gather round."

"Fireworks in the pants?"

"Ten dollars that dick is brimming with chlamydia."

"Twenty on herpes."

"Let's see—hold up—oh hello, genital rash!"

"That's it? I'm kind of disappointed, to be honest."

"Who's on Angry Santa? The vitals aren't gonna check themselves."

"I hope Angry Santa learns to drive that sleigh better."

"I hope they take away his license."

Rudd had pretended to sleep while the blood-pressure cuff tightened and sizzed.

A NON-NURSE VOICE SAID, "Are you okay?"

"Hanh?" He thrashed awake, found himself in a chair in the sunroom. Caz stood in front of him in a tiny black jumper.

"Hi, Mr. Rudd. Do you want some help getting to the dining room?"

"Not on your sweet life," he said, gripping the walker and pulling himself to standing. The notecards fell out of his lap. Caz gathered them from the floor and tucked them into his jacket pocket. "Cheers," he muttered. She really did have nice tits.

Lasko poked his head in. "Hey, could you help? Addie's just refusing. Sorry."

"Do you know what upset her?" Caz said.

"Nothing specific that I can tell. Although, I mean, why do *any* of us get into a mood, right?"

Adeline's Room

"HEY THERE." CAZ SMILED toward Adeline. "You ready for lunch?"

Adeline shook her head, clutching Bashy.

"Let's go, okay?"

"But Mama," Adeline said.

"Did she have her Ensure this morning?"

"Spat out most of it," Lasko said.

Adeline squeezed Bashy harder. "Mama."

"I'm Caz."

"Where's the take-the-picture thing?"

Caz looked at Lasko, who said, "Camera."

"We don't have a camera here, other than our phones—do we?"

"No but we could get one," he said. "Would you be into that, Adeline? Should we buy a real proper camera?"

Adeline narrowed her eyes.

"Let's go eat," Caz said, grateful that Lasko had more patience than she did.

Dining Room

AT THE TABLE by the kitchen doors, Kestrel posed a community question: "If you could write and direct a horror movie, what would it be called? I'll start: *The Dicks Have Eyes.*"

Ant: "*The Dicks Have Eyes 2: The Dangling.*"

Rudd: "Jesus God, who just ripped one off?"

"Smelt it, dealt it," Kestrel said.

"This one ought to be hospitalized soon as."

"Soon as what?"

"Bloody possible," Rudd said.

"You are a ray of Chernobyl sunshine," Kestrel said.

"Ray of common *sense.*"

"Dream on, you wrankled scrotum."

"San fairy Ann," Rudd said.

"Ça ne fait rien," Ant said.

"Hanh?"

"French for 'doesn't matter.' British soldiers in World War I brought back an Anglicized version of the phrase, which you, apparently, learned."

"Oh aye?"

"Why do you know that?"

Ant gave Mrs. Quimbee a long, dry look. "Because Black people go to college, too?"

"It's not a racial thing. I'm just surprised that this obscure fact about the First World War—"

"It *is* a racial thing," Ant said, "but you do you."

"Now that I think about it," Rudd said, "back in the day, when a bloke got rejected by a woman—sexually, you know—we used to call that a French bench. So that's another influence of France."

"What does that mean, 'you do you'?" Mrs. Quimbee said.

"It means 'shut up,'" Rudd said. His granny had told him that when the war ended the Spanish flu was just getting started, and it killed more people than the war did. There was a neighbor family in West Riding whose five children all died from it. The sickness ran remorselessly through the asylum where she worked. "Maybe you've heard of a little book called *Wuthering Heights*?" he added to no one in particular. "That's where I'm from."

"I seem to have become everyone's punching bag!" Mrs. Quimbee said.

"Everything okay over there?" Caz called from the other table.

"Only the usual rudeness," Mrs. Quimbee shouted back.

"Your husband had the shiniest lips," Caz said.

"They weren't that shiny," Vara said.

"Oh, they were *so* shiny! Pass me the water?"

Davey chomped the not-salty-enough chicken, his forehead throbbing from the shrieks of the boy, who was running around all hyper as fuck. The boy's sister in her discount jeans reminded Davey of someone. A girl from Bagram? No: this girl was white as hell, the color of inner potato.

"I want to hear more about your band," he told Caz. "Like, how it came to be."

"It came to be because I was bored. And boring."

He cracked his knuckles. "You could never be boring."

"I was just this typical girl," Caz said, "and did I mind? Yes. So I bought a guitar. I ended up playing bass, because Vara was better at guitar, but—"

"How were you ever typical?"

"Believe me, I was a dime a dozen. At least I would've been, if I'd kept doing what I was supposed to do."

"But you didn't," Davey said. "Maybe that's why you're still so freaking sexy."

She gave him the finger.

Watching them, Nola decided that Caz was Blanche. (Kestrel had been the first Blanche contender.) Mrs. Quimbee was Rose. Marika was Sophia. Caz and Vara both had elements of Dorothy, but Vara had more. Caz was less grounded, more distracted. She didn't seem to remember that Nola had been at the House before— last Wednesday, when the music class gave a performance. Nola remembered all of it: the school bus stopping at the end of North Street, seventh graders pouring out, October wind stinging their faces. They'd been told their singing would bring joy to the dying. They felt glad not to be dying. The room they were led into had eight walls instead of four, which struck them as mysterious. Caz told them the room had once held a gigantic aquarium.

The children arranged themselves on the staircase overlooking the couches and stone hearth and fraying little rugs. A man with a long forehead, fist on his walker, had pointed at the children and bellowed, "Warm homes, warm food!" Finger stabbing his own chest: "Cold home, cold food." "Is that Frankenstein?" a kid said. "Okay everyone," Caz said, adjusting a buttock on the piano bench, "this song is called 'Halloween.'" Two dozen banshees opened their mouths.

Nola had snuck away from the back row mid-song, up the rest of the stairs, to the second floor. A dog had followed her along the hall while voices surged from below: "Trick or treat! Trick or treat! The bitter and the sweet." The dog growled and pawed at

Nola's stern brown brogan, a shoe she never would have picked for herself.

"See what the place is like," Stell had instructed her on the phone, the day before. "See if there's enough room."

IN THE AUTUMN OF 1945, a second lieutenant in the US Army had looked through the witch window at the pines and thought of eating horsemeat in Belgium, wrestling with his lover (another lieutenant) under a filthy blanket; and he had feared he would never know joy so deep again. They'd been sent to the mountains, a handful of soldiers who might recover, to a private family home turned into a convalescent hospital. It was better than the army hospital in that there was less screaming and more food. The second lieutenant was amazed to encounter a land-house so like a sea-house, as though a wave had dropped a boat onto a cliff where, waiting for another wave to carry it off, it sank a little deeper each year into the dirt. It was too awkwardly shaped to be beautiful and not large enough to be grand, but he liked it here.

When he was able to walk outside, with a nurse, he found the grounds unremarkable but for one well-tended grave: "BELOVED WIFE." The flowers looked fresh. He asked who brought them, who cleaned the headstone. The nurse didn't know.

When they went back inside she sat him by the oriel window and administered the daily egg, holding a cup at his shaking lips to tip the yolk down his throat.

"Shame about the floor," the nurse said, poking one white-shoed toe at a gash in the hardwood.

THE GASH WAS A HOLE in the Fish Bowl floor, and it was Vara's frustration that it hadn't been fixed, and it was a wartime nurse's shyness around the men she took care of, and it was the sea captain's restless despair—all at once, alone and together.

Library

JAMES KNELT ON THE WINDOW seat, nose pressed to the cold glass pane. When he drew back from the window, his eyes could focus on the other side of it: black trees, white ground, air slashed by brash flakes. Somewhere beyond the trees was his mama. *Sleep, sleep, our little fur child. Out of the windiness, out of the wild.* One more night, Nola had said. It was always one more night. When would there be no more nights? He felt so frustrated he banged the pane with his palm, then with his forehead. It was possible that Mama wasn't coming to find him but was waiting, beyond the trees, for him to find her.

Vara's Bathroom

THE BLUNT PRESSURE under her spine-root had been building, her last shit days ago. She maneuvered herself onto the toilet and bore down. It was bunched right there at the opening, she could feel it swelling and ready, but it refused. She propped her elbow on the sink. Strained more. Something flared, a hard pop of pain. "Fuck!" she shouted, but no shit came.

Fronzi padded into the bathroom. Stared up at her.

"Nothing," Vara said, "just some torn inner ass-flesh."

Like trying to shit a sugar bowl.

She took a break to muster strength. The dog lay in a crescent at her bare feet. In one of the murder shows, detectives had found a man dead on the toilet with his heart burst like a tomato. Imagine them telling her children. Imagine her children telling their friends, "Actually, she died on the toilet."

Vara clenched every muscle she could think of. Come on, asshole, a few more millimeters!

Like trying to shit a cantaloupe.

The warmer it got, the more mosquitoes would hatch.

She rose and waddled, panties ankled, to clutch the bathroom doorframe, where she hoped gravity might dislodge it. It was *right there*, so close. Fronzi barked, and Vara coughed—would coughing help? She thumped back down on the toilet. Her shredded ass couldn't compete with the white-heat hurt of childbirth, but it helped to think of that, since labor had an end, couldn't just go on forever as this felt like it might. All her thrusting and huffing and lung-wrenching heaves had pushed only a few clumped grains out of the opening, where they hung tantalizingly, a tip of the bigger load.

Half an hour she guessed it had been. No more fingering the fecal tip: she needed to dig and grip. She shoved one finger into the tender pocket. The turd was knobby, as if a string of beads had been abandoned in there to grow bloated and crusty. She pushed her thumb in, too, and fought to get a tweezing leverage. New hurt screamed up when she tugged.

After she had wiped herself and maneuvered from the toilet to her bed, Vara thought about Ant, a few doors down the hall, writing their dissertation. Maybe she could ask to read it? Vara had once imagined herself embarking on such a project, something long and difficult and electrifying; she would have written a thesis if she'd stayed in college. The top spot on her revenge list had been occupied for more than forty years by an assistant professor who, as they were walking out of the building after class, had said "You're such a beautiful girl" and kissed her on the mouth. The sidewalk had been crowded, and everyone could see. They were kissing on the sidewalk and then the assistant professor was pressing Vara against a stone wall and then they were lying in a grove of trees. She was making decisions, or declining to make them, from somewhere outside her body; watching herself get led; knowing she did not want to do this, or most of her didn't. The part that did want to said, "You can't tell me not to!" even if he was not handsome, even if his mouth was rubbery and whispered phrases ("I'm a bad boy, aren't I? Such a bad boy!") that made Vara want to laugh. She had gone along with it. On the grass between tall trees, the assistant professor told her to squeeze his ass. "I bet you've got spectacular tits, don't you." Begged her to lick his nipple. She squeezed; she licked. Once the pants were off and he was hard on her leg and she had tilted her hips for his dick to get in, once his dick was in and he was jerking to and fro, once he started to wheeze—she detached from the moment. She knew it was happening, but she was not involved.

His remarks about how smart she was. The gushing praise for her essays. "You should be my TA next year!" Had it all been complete bullshit? *You're such a beautiful girl.*

She hadn't been able to tell her parents why she was dropping out of college—how the shame of having sex with the assistant professor had kept her in her dorm room for days, eating nothing but saltines, telling herself over and over how stupid she was—so she'd faked an illness severe enough for a leave of absence that turned out to be permanent. It was 1977 and nobody was going to get too upset if a girl did not finish college. At least, nobody Vara knew. She phoned the thrift shop where Caz worked and said, "Can we get drunk?" and Caz said, "Indeed we can," then asked if Vara wanted to be in the band Caz was starting. "It's going to be all girls," Caz added, "and all magic."

Kitchen

THE DISHWASHER HAD been making a new sound, and Lasko was worried, but he didn't want to think about it—he hated to see in a worry the shape of its future, to watch it get cruel and enormous—so he concentrated on washing the cast-iron pot. Kestrel, assigned to help with Sunday lunch cleanup, was sitting at the long table, on her phone, poring over the socials of the bar. (The hot bartender's personal account was set to private.)

"You're like having a brother who is much nicer than my actual brothers," she told Lasko.

"And you're like my sister." But he didn't mean it the whole way.

Caz came in and wetted a dish towel and pressed it over her eyes. "Are these sugar-free?" She reached into a pan of cookie-dough ghosts. "There's a weird aftertaste."

"There's raw egg in it," Lasko warned. "How many times in its life do you think this pot has been washed?"

Caz peeked out from under the towel. "That was my grand-mother's, so—thousands? At least one thousand."

Lasko set the clean pot on a low flame.

"Won't it burn?"

"How have you gone sixty-whatever years without learning cast-iron care?" Lasko said.

Kestrel raised the sheet pan off the counter. "Can we start baking these?"

"It's not quite all the way preheated, but sure. Here, give." Lasko slid the pan into the oven. His parents had taught him not to take up too much space, because his parents had believed he was a girl.

"When I get promoted at WikiWhattheFuck," Kestrel said, "I'm getting an enameled cast-iron Le Creuset."

"You don't even cook."

"As soon as I own a Le Creuset Dutch oven in flame or artichoke, I will. And some mini-cocottes. They're extremely adorable. Are you taking notes? Christmas is coming. I want a set of mini-cocottes for my secret Santa."

"If it's under twenty-five dollars, it's yours."

"Can you even buy a fart for under twenty-five dollars?" Kestrel said.

Dish towel wadded on top of her head, Caz opened the fridge. "Your generation lacks imagination. Speaking of farts." Closed the fridge. "Tell Lasko your latest preferred adjectives for them."

"Oh my God!" Kestrel said. "Well, *currently* my favorites include 'tawny,' 'hammy,' 'brute,' and 'hollering.'"

"Mine," Caz said, "are 'moany,' 'jammy,' and 'fugue-like.'"

"She's also partial," Kestrel whispered to Lasko, "to 'laden' and 'hushed.'"

"Fair enough," he said. To hide his hot red face, he went out to snip some mint. He had a cold frame in back, his tiny holding, where he grew the common herbs for cooking and a few less common ones for tea—bergamot, sweet woodruff, dittany of Crete. Almost everything had died already, but mint was a baller. Even in this weather he could still get a few good leaves. Mint was Vara's favorite. Marika liked lapsang souchong, and Mr. Rudd liked PG Tips. Caz and Kestrel only drank coffee.

Nola ran into the kitchen, frowning. "Excuse me, is James in here?"

"You'd hear him if he was," Lasko said.

"Try the library," Caz said.

"I already did. The library and the Fish Bowl and the hall. I was just—I was in the bathroom. Not even for that long."

"It's okay, he's around somewhere."

Nola clutched her chin with both hands, pulling at the skin, exposing the gumline of her bottom teeth. "Please will you help me find him?"

HE WASN'T IN THE DINING ROOM or the Fish Bowl. He wasn't in the office or the library; he wasn't on the back porch. Lasko checked all the bathrooms, and Mrs. Quimbee checked the phone nook, and Vara checked every corner of the infirmary. Mr. Rudd slept on a chair in the sunroom. Adeline slept under the whale quilt. Caz and Davey went from bedroom to bedroom, looking for the boy (and, in Davey's case, for orange prescription bottles) while Ant and Fronzi stomped through the snowdrifts around the House perimeter. Marika watched from the window of her bedroom. Kestrel held Nola in her arms.

Marika's Room

SHE NEEDED TO STAY at the window in case he came into view. It was possible to see things from this window that no one else could. She might be able to spot James down there, in the trees, in the snow. It was so cold out he must have been freezing by now, his small toes turning black, eyelashes hardening to ice. She couldn't do much but she could keep watch and stand vigil and yell her loudest when she saw him so the others would know.

She had not been loud when her brother got shot: it had happened before she could open her mouth, which was full of half-chewed artichoke. By the time she had swallowed, Theo was dead.

Wolves swallowed poison lichen and broken glass tucked into reindeer carcasses.

Bells on a collar, bright clanking distraction, split their attention until the strays could catch up and the herd was restored—one body made of nineteen bodies unbreachable in the mountain sun. Wolf bells. The necessary noise.

Because shoelace.

Because eyelashes.

Because ghee-ah.

Because he was a little bear.

What if this boy, too, never came back?

Marika's grandmother had stopped wearing the bells a few months before she gave birth to her first son. That son would father four children. One of the children would be shot on the floor of their house; two would be killed in a death camp; one would be a refugee, a student, an architect, a milk-hater, a watcher of murder shows.

A dolphin with an anchor, Marika suddenly remembered, meant *spevde vradeos*. "Make haste slowly." Fuck that adage! They needed haste and fire—they needed noise. There were no bells to wear, only the blue dress and the underpants that smelled like the putrefied apples in her closet. Why should she bother with these useless garments? Why should she wear any clothes at all?

Kitchen

NOLA WASN'T A KNIFE. She was a blob who had lost James. She had lied about only being in the bathroom for a few minutes: she'd been fast asleep on the library couch. Hadn't Lasko been watching him? She'd figured *someone* was around—that was the beauty, after all, of a house like this, that someone always was— but she'd been wrong. *Was* wrong. Was a sad wrong fuck who had failed.

It would be so much easier if . . .

One of Nola's enduring fears was that her thoughts would somehow leak out of her brain and hang legible on the air in smoke-colored letters. She had gone so far as to ask the science teacher if it could happen. "Not in *this* world," the science teacher had said. In what world, then, were such horrors possible?

It would be so much easier if—

No one could hear her, but still . . .

—I didn't have to worry about him.

The problem was not that James was autistic. The problem was that society wasn't built for him. Nola's body digested food easily, fell asleep easily, and could sit still for long stretches of time. Her head didn't mind hats. Her eyes didn't mind sharp lights. She could keep quiet when she was supposed to. Her mouth translated her thoughts into sounds other people recognized. Her ears decoded the words other people said at the same speed they were saying them. She hated gym and math, and was not an avid reader, but she didn't get stowed in a trailer by the soccer field with the other kids they didn't know what to do with.

The world itself was the reason she had to worry.

JAMES WALKED AMONG THE TREES, his bare feet burning. The air was making circles on his cheek, pushing the wetness back into his eyes, and shivering his spine, and he loved it. He wanted this cold to never stop. He thought about Mama. If he walked long enough, would he find her? Above him the reaching trees, their slow quiet; below him the white snow hot on his white feet. Hottest on the arches. He wanted Mama here to stop the burning. He wanted to rise up into the trees, to be lifted from the snow and feel unburned in the quiet. In most houses it was never quiet. He hated shoes on his feet—they squeezed and bit and cut off the air—but this snow also hurt and when would Mama be here?

Black trees, green trees, white feet hurting under the quiet, and he loved the trees standing with him and he loved his Mama. Shreds of snow floated down onto more snow, deep-burning. He said "Mama" into the quiet, lifting one foot then the other, but he couldn't keep both in the air at once. Mama was the person he could be most quiet with, and he missed her, and his feet burned against the floor of this palace of trees.

A man was coming toward him in a puffy bright-red jacket saying, "Well hi there, buddy! You lost?"

He waited.

"You must be freezing, son. Letsgetyoustraightinside. Is it okay if I pick you up?"

James knuckle-tapped his chin. The man reached down. In his arms, there was no more burning.

Marika's Room

HER GRANDMOTHER HAD gone out with the flock carrying a leather-sheathed knife and a rock sling made of braided wool. She'd worn brass bells around her wrists and ankles, shaking them at the wolves if they came. A wolf was more than one thing: parent, mate, runner of meadows, drinker of water from spring-fed streams. But to her grandmother, terrified on a mountainside, the wolf would have been only one thing. Marika herself would have wanted a gun.

Front Hall

THE DOORBELL RANG.

It was Pastor Jeff, holding James. "I think you lost someone." He set the boy down and Caz reached for him, but James ran off, chirping irritably, toward the kitchen. "Found him over by the property line. I was taking my afternoon walk when who shows up but this rascal."

From the kitchen came a burst of cheers.

"He wasn't wearing any shoes," the pastor said.

"He doesn't like shoes."

"Plenty of things we don't like in this world, but we have to tolerate them. He could've gotten frostbite."

Dutiful goddamn lamb of God. "Well, thanks for bringing him back," she said. "We'll take good care of him."

"I know you want to," he said, smiling and frowning at the same time. "You have a generous heart, Caz. All that you're doing with this House—it's wonderful! We're proud to have you as neighbors. And I'd love to help you out with these kiddos. Obviously they can't stay here with you, so why don't I reach out to CPS—I've got a friend who works there—and figure out a better plan?"

"Well, they *could* stay here."

"Could they? Really?"

"Why the fuck not?" she said.

"All the studies show that little ones benefit from living with two parents. Mother and father. But we don't need studies to tell us what we already know—it's just common sense. The stability of the family is what gives children roots, and what makes their wings grow strong. I want that for *these* children, don't you?"

"Do I want them to grow wings?"

Pastor Jeff chuckled. "I know the metaphor is trite. But a lot of trite things happen to be true. And this is such a serious problem. You've got addicts leaving drugs out on the coffee table and their toddlers eat them and overdose, and if they survive the overdose they get removed from the home, which of course they should, but then CPS can't figure out what to do with them. The foster system is so overloaded—it has been for years—and they simply can't handle the need. There is so much *need*, Caz. Children shouldn't have to suffer because of an underfunded bureaucracy. This is where my congregation steps in. We can place kids with church families without all the paperwork and incompetent case management and database errors."

"Is that even legal?"

"It can be, yes! The child's parent or guardian has to sign off, of course. There's plenty of precedent for this, and my friend at CPS knows the ropes. In the case of James and Nola, we'd just have to—"

"How do you know their names?"

His face flashed with businesslike contempt, a boss growing impatient with a dawdling subordinate. "From the amber alert. Look, I'm only thinking of what's best for them. We have one family in particular, longtime church members, who would be willing to welcome a child with special needs. They want to step up and care for the least among us."

Caz slammed the door in his face.

THE CAPTAIN HAD thrown a hammer across the room because the mountains depressed him. His children bored him. He missed his wife and missed the sea, tall ships with every sail shaking. The housekeeper had seen him throw it. Accustomed by then to his scrotum-spraying and his habit of speaking to the grave in the garden, she was not shocked.

Second-Floor Bathroom

"**WE NEED TO GET YOU WARM** again!" Vara said.

Lasko tested the water with his wrist, then squirted bubble bath into the gush from the tap. "Climb on in."

"Ghee-ah ghee-ah ghee-ah," James said, smiling at him.

Vara backed her chair up against the sink, and Lasko sat on the wall of the tub while James splashed. The water seemed to relax him, though he was still wriggling a lot, getting up, sitting down. Whenever he stood, dripping with soap, Vara saw his penis and thought about when her own boy was young—the cuteness of those tiny fleshy acorns, unthreatening yet. Like a thumb-sized accordion, James's retracted or elongated depending on his posture. He sat, lowered his face into the froth of bubbles, and when he came back up Lasko said, "Well hello, Santa Claus!"

The boy stood again and shouted.

"You ready to get out already?"

He tapped his chin yes.

Lasko pulled a towel off the rack. "Okay then, come on." James climbed cautiously from the tub, one leg at a time, into his waiting arms.

Marika said from the doorway: "How is he?"

Lasko squatted to dry James's legs. "He seems fine."

Vara rubbed calendula into the welts on his wrists.

"Are any of those potted plants downstairs poisonous? Because he's been eating them. Or at least putting them in his mouth."

"I have no idea," Vara said.

The boy squirmed out of Lasko's towel-hug.

"But you're a nurse," Marika said.

"Not a gardener."

"I'm kind of a gardener," Lasko said, "but I don't know, either. I can look it up."

"Good." Marika took James's hand. "I'll get him dressed."

"Oh, no, you don't need—"

"Let's go, mílo mou!"

Like she had some special claim, Vara thought.

Library

NOLA SAT ON THE LEATHER COUCH with her arms clasping her folded knees, gaze resting on a tumbling slash of pink in the mostly dark-green carpet. He wasn't lost. She hadn't lost him. He was upstairs and breathing and safe.

"Hey, Miss Nola." Caz plunked herself down on the couch. "He doesn't seem any the worse for wear. What a relief, right?"

If she tried to speak she would start crying, so Nola just nodded.

"It'll be time to eat soon. Would you come help me get Adeline squared away? She likes to have her hair brushed before dinner."

Many of the books that had been read to Nola when she was younger took place on other planets, or in the star-dotted air between planets; and her small self had conceived of outer space as a realm free from disappointment, where things were wondrous all the time. This moment was like those books.

She followed Caz into the hall, dazed and exultant. She was a knife again. An architect of debris.

Rudd's Room

MR. RUDD WAS STARTING A NOTE to Georgina when James came in and went to the window and peered out, shoelace whirling. He liked this window because of its tree: silver and blue and black and leaning.

"Just gonna barge into anyone's room, are you, little shiverthewink?"

"Baaahhhh," James said.

"Oh aye?" Rudd said.

The boy gave him the side-eye.

"Charm to spare, you. Want a bit of this?" He held out a slice of parkin, which James pushed away. "Your loss," Rudd said, then wrote on the notecard: "Sweet George, guess what, they baked me my own pan of parkin! That cook is nicer than I credited him for. Love, Your Dad."

Georgie had tried to be casual about her surgery. Played up the historical angle. The Amazons, she'd told him, would burn off their left breasts to better carry their shields, or their right breasts to better aim their nocked arrows. He remembered listening to his daughter talk about Amazon breasts in the phone nook, amid the garble of the Fish Bowl TV, wondering how it would feel to scorch your own tit off.

But she wasn't dead.

But yes she was.

But why did that have to be true?

"Hello?" came a hoarse cry from the hall. "Mr. Rudd, may I enter?"

"Suit yourself."

In rolled Mrs. Quimbee, grinning like the maniac she was. On her lap was an orange contraption with black-and-white keys, like a tiny piano.

"I wanted to see if the boy might enjoy this," Quimbee said, handing the thing to Rudd. "Could you put it on the desk for him?"

Rudd obliged.

"Look at the keyboard, James!" Quimbee said. "Do you like it?"

James remained at the window, staring out.

Rudd pressed one of the fat plastic keys.

"You have to turn it on," Quimbee said. "The switch at the back."

Now it made a sound: tinkly, bright. "Hear that, shiverthewink? You can play your own songs."

James kept his gaze on the trees.

"I thought he would like it," Quimbee said.

"Can't force these things."

"I bought it for my grandson last Christmas, before I found out he already had one. I didn't have the energy to return it." She fussed at the top button of her cardigan. "Well, perhaps in time he'll take an interest."

"Want some gingerbread?" Rudd said. "Best I've tasted outside of Yorkshire."

"Only a very small piece," she said.

Adeline's Room

ADELINE HEARD THE BELL, a fretful chime, and the horse wouldn't run—beaten, even, he wouldn't—because he had tapeworm from the raining and all of him was weak, and Adeline was becalmed in refeeling, every horse-pain repeating in the dark of her throat.

In the green chair, her attention was on floating faces, chair green, air watery, feet heavy on the floor, and the faces—her mother's, Grandfather's, the uncles'—fierce in the room with her. Her mother eyeless and lipless, a flesh mound with nostrils; the uncles two red ovals; Grandfather asleep. Some days (the easy days) no faces, but today faces. Here on the curtains, on the ceiling, here in the dust on the window's white sill. Tiny sounds of faces. Her feet so heavy no chance of escape. The horses? Gone. The horses unreal. Made of painted rubber. How, then, alive? Sweet, nurbling sounds of horses here, true alive horses, not toys. Dead faces in the room with her. Dark branches outside desiring inside. Adeline here, and the horses, and the faces, and soon dinner. What foods tonight? Lasagna terrible always. Fish okay. Carrots not enough salt. Cook sweet but clumsy with salt. Slow with the water-boiling.

Salt in the dish instead of sugar, mouth in pain, greedy girls needed punishment—salt-mouth worse than spanking, but spanked, too. Small and weeping and sent up without dinner. Sweet true horses. A hard gallop, hard spanking, no salt, branches scratching. Not in here, branches. Not when faces mouthless and eyeless. Mother-face, uncle-face, horse-face. Face in the window Adeline's. A friend, this window, staring for days. Cold in the dinner room. Bad windows there. Her own good thick window. Klootchy

the kangaroo a hater of cold, but Bashy the porcupine fine with it.
Two faces always here: her mother's and hers. Uncles sometimes,
and Grandfather sometimes—smell of cologne and pipe tobacco,
bookshelves and saddles, the song about a harbor-haunting mermaid. No cruel remarks allowed around Grandfather. Nothing
about unmarried sluts. Thank you, Grandfather. After his death:
banishment. The uncles so cruel. House to be turned into a bed
and breakfast, no space for them. *But I can work! I'll clean the
rooms!* but uncles firm: *Nope.* Adeline in the tunnel, hiding. When
found, spanked hard, the hardest in her life.

"Miss Adeline? You ready to eat?" It was her daughter in the
room now, and her daughter's daughter.

But her daughter had no daughter.

Bashy the porcupine with her, tucked, but hair unbrushed. Inch
of white in the furrow of her part. "No—"

"What can I help with?" Caz said.

I'll clean the rooms!

Her daughter's daughter, brushing, said, "Like that?" The bris-
tles beautiful on her skull. Forever, this feeling.

Her face in the window-mirror too vague to see. Hair probably
looking awful, needing to be dyed again soon. *I can work! I'll
clean the rooms!*

"Shall we go?" her daughter said.

Adeline's mouth muscles not listening. Bashy the porcupine,
instead, held up to mean "yes."

Dining Room

TOO NAUSEATED TO EAT, Vara spent dinner ignoring Adeline's remarks about the horses who had once lived at the House. She was assembling a pile of nondairy creamers for upstairs when a Dracula giggle came from the kitchen, Caz prancing through the doors, Davey on her heels. Handsome and Gretel.

"Can we sit with you?"

"I'm finished." Vara backed away from the table and aimed her chair toward the hall door.

"Then have some more tea. It's not like you're going anywhere."

"I can smell the cigarette you just had."

"Congratulations." Caz still standing, hips jutting.

"Killing yourself," Vara murmured.

"What?"

"She said you're killing yourself!" Davey boomed.

"I'd hate to see an X-ray of *your* lungs," Vara told him. "Did you know it'd been almost three decades since she quit smoking? Was that little fact conveyed during pillow talk? And yet suddenly, under your influence, she starts again."

He crossed his arms, pushing out the biceps muscles with his knuckles. "Are you on some kind of medication that makes you a dick?"

"I was a dick long before medication," Vara said. She tried to open a creamer to sip, but her hands weren't cooperating, the tiny tab on the cover was too small to get a purchase on, the container jumped out of her hands and onto the floor and Caz started to pick it up but Vara yelled "No!" and started throwing every creamer in her lap at the wall. One burst open on impact. The flung drops were brief flowers, then a streaking, on the flocked green.

"The wall's crying," Adeline said.

Vara steered herself out of the dining room.

Caz scratched her leg.

Davey clicked two spoons together: "Four, three, two, one . . . There's a hole in daddy's arm where all the money goes! Something something, something something . . . with a purple heart and a monkey on his back."

"Just like you," Caz said, "minus the purple heart."

"I never shot up, though."

"And you're not a daddy."

"Well."

"What?"

Davey shrugged.

"You are?"

"He's about the same age as little man," nodding over at James, who was donkey-kicking the kitchen doors. "Lives out East with his mom."

"There's a hole," Adeline said.

"Wow," Caz said, "that's—wow." A lot of people in the world had children. But *Davey*?

Ant plucked the napkin out of Caz's hand. "You just wiped your mouth on that."

"But my glasses are all . . ."

"And smearing them with meaty saliva," Ant said, "will help how?"

Caz used her sweatshirt sleeve instead.

Davey started dancing next to James, mirroring his kicks and his wiggling fingers.

Vara's Room

SHE DIDN'T ALLOW HERSELF to cry until she was safely inside, door locked, Fronzi glad to see her. "It's okay," she told the dog, "I'm just . . ." What was she? Mad? Sad? Lonely? Drained, she decided. It was the least humiliating word she could think of.

Once Caz found someone for the CNA position, Vara would no longer have to hand out meds in the morning, or dictate chart notes about Mr. Rudd's urinary tract infections, or order salve for Marika's skin. She would no longer be pestered by Mrs. Quimbee about the shapes of various moles. Caz kept saying how much she wanted Vara to be free from responsibility—how much she wanted her to *rest*—but Caz couldn't understand the satisfaction of carrying out these tasks.

Or maybe she could. Vara hadn't tried to tell her.

Monster from the mind of Mary W.
castle-bound, unsound
the volcano took the sun
and the rain won't stop
so she writes & writes & writes

"Freezing Summer," their one true hit, had been born in Arkansas. The show the night before was in a basement, ten pale kids watching, unmoved, before marching back upstairs. Nobody bought a tape. Not worth coming, but you had to come. The next morning they were tired and their mouths tasted like moss. They drove past the high school into which the 101st Airborne Division had escorted the Little Rock Nine. The Black students had been screamed at, spat on, threatened with death, attacked in bathrooms with burning toilet paper. A white boy had thrown acid into their eyes. When Vara saw the school she thought about how little it mattered what she was doing with her life compared with what those nine teenagers had done in 1957.

Bolts' first drummer (Vara couldn't remember her name—she hadn't lasted long) parallel-parked the van near a diner. She was a better driver than drummer, that much Vara did recall. People on the street, as usual, stared. At the diner entrance stood guys who looked like Archie comics characters. "Hey there, lezzes."

"Oh my God, hi!" Caz shouted.

Vara slowed, bracing for worse.

"Screw you, vampire," a guy said.

Caz widened her eyes and did a Dracula laugh while Vara and the first drummer hurried inside to the relief of a booth protecting their bodies from other bodies. Vara was the only Asian person in the restaurant.

They ordered fried eggs and fried ham. The first drummer went to find the bathroom.

"When we're old," Caz said, "can we live in the same nursing home?"

Vara peeled the lid off a nondairy creamer and tipped it into her mouth. "Yeah, adjoining rooms."

"I'm serious."

"Me too." She tore open another tiny white container.

"You'll get cancer," Caz said.

"I'd have to drink five million."

"Well, you already drank three million." Caz lit a cigarette. "So it's a pact?"

"Unless we're enemies by then," Vara said, "or have husbands. This ham is delicious."

"I won't have a husband," Caz said.

"You don't know that."

"I do know that." She blew smoke in Vara's face.

"This is the best ham I've ever tasted."

The first drummer came back, dripping.

"Fucking *why*," Caz said, "do you never dry your hands?"

"It wastes paper and I personally choose not to help kill the planet."

Vara, the peacekeeper back then: "How far is the drive to Memphis?"

"A drop got in my *eye!*"

"Two and a half hours," the first drummer said, shoveling acid-yellow eggs into her mouth. "I can't believe Elvis died. Now there's no hope."

"Were you planning to fuck him?"

"Caz, *God*." Vara closed her eyes. "So loud."

"What? Every person in this diner already hates us."

Caz had loved the glory of being despised. Yet, Vara thought, she would never feel, upon walking into a room, that the white people in the room believed she had less of a right to be in the room than they did. Caz would never know what that felt like.

"He got gross at the end," the first drummer said, "but even so, I would've ridden that cock."

"Climate change is cyclical," Caz said, picking a brown shred from her lip. "You have to look at history. Drastic temperature fluctuations have always—"

"You're wrong, actually." The first drummer yawned too much and instead of tampons she used wedges of sea sponge and left them crusting on the toilet tank, but Vara had loved her when she corrected Caz.

"Then how," said Caz, who in any year would have breezed into Little Rock High safe and sound, "do you account for the summer of 1816? There was frost in August!"

"I don't know," the first drummer said. "Pterodactyls?"

"Famine broke out all across the northern hemisphere," Caz said. "They called it 'Freezing Summer.' Which." She grinned. "Isn't the worst name for a song."

"Nor is it the best," the drummer said.

Caz had looked at Vara and slowly dragged her index finger across her throat.

She used to make you feel special, as long as you did what she wanted. *You're the only one who's there for me. You're the only one who gets it.* You were rewarded if you said what she wanted to hear. Those who dared to tell her the truth, meanwhile: *That fucking bitch fucked me over, she's the worst person alive, he betrayed me, he can suck my clit, I hope he fucking dies.* If you didn't help her fast enough—lend her money soon enough—if you didn't drop everything and do her bidding, oh, the rage! Vara used to fantasize about retorts (her favorite was *You know where I'm not at? Your beck and call*) but could never bring herself to say them. She was quiet while Caz ranted. She stood by while Caz flailed. She kept her face calm when Caz called her boring and prudish and depressed and judgmental.

For years, she took it.

Then she told Caz she was engaged to be married and was quitting the band. Caz said it was the ultimate sabotage, that Vara was betraying their feminist principles, surrendering to the patriarchy, that she was ruining the best thing that had ever happened to either of them, and that she would never speak to Vara again. "That's fine with me," Vara had said, and meant it.

Now, to stop her mind, she did the most mindless thing within reach—applied lipstick—and said to the mirror: "A young lady is finished."

"Vara?" Kestrel's voice from the hall. "Is the dog with you?" Once inside the room she cried, "Check *you* out in the come-fuck-me lippy!"

"That is not the message I'm sending," Vara said.

"You may not be sending it, but we're *receiving* it. It legit looks fabulous."

"Is that supposed to make my day?"

"Uhh-*um*? I was giving you a compliment, that's all. But I need to walk this little lady. Come on, Fronz." Fronzi didn't move from Vara's unslept-side pillow, which Kestrel seemed to take as permission to delay or perhaps altogether skip the walk. "So what kind of lipstick is it?"

"I don't bother knowing. I wear cosmetics maliciously now."

Kestrel found the tube on the dresser. "'Diamond Hoof.' *What?*"

"They ran out of good lipstick names a long time ago."

"You really do look amazing in that color."

"The problem with compliments," Vara said, "is that you're supposed to be grateful for them, even though they're reinforcing the idea that a woman's value lies in how she looks."

"I think we've moved beyond that stage of feminism."

"Moved beyond?"

"It's just that everyone kind of knows that by now. It's like saying the sky is blue."

"You remind me of my daughter," Vara said. "When she was

planning her wedding, I told her that women didn't march and strike and get arrested so that she could make monogrammed towels her highest ambition, and she said excuse me for not being sufficiently oppressed. Zero awareness of history. Or, frankly, of the present moment."

"Wow, thanks." Kestrel yanked Fronzi by the collar off the bed. "If I'm not aware of the past or the present, I guess it's good I have plenty of future."

Vara kept her eyes closed until she heard the door slam.

Then it opened again. "I'm sorry, that was bitchy."

"It was."

After a few seconds Kestrel added, "You were being kind of bitchy, too."

"Do you hear shrieking?"

"Uh-*umm*?" Kestrel cocked her head. "Yeah, that might be shrieking."

All the Rooms

JAMES DIDN'T WANT to be here. Why was he still here? He was running, he was reaching, he was dancing his fingers to calm down his eyes. Opened a door but once through the door he wasn't sure where to go. He ran down the stairs, ran up the stairs, ran down again, tearful and wailing, pleading for relief. Someone was shouting "What is it?" and "Stop!" and someone was chasing him, but they wouldn't catch him. He was hunting, panicky, and the hunted object kept changing: the kitchen doors, his shoelace, a cup of water, the plants, his shoelace, Nola's shoulder, the stairs. Nothing gave him relief for more than three seconds. He hated that Nola hadn't figured out how to go back to Mama. She needed to figure it out, because he couldn't. They needed to go back right now, because when was soon? Soon, he feared, was never. He wanted away from these too-loud rooms, his eyes hurt, his wrists itched, he wanted a hard surface to feel against, and Mama when was soon? When it got to be soon he'd go away, hard-far from every loud place, from every itch, from everything that bothered his eyes. He hated this sensation in his eyes, he wanted soon to be exactly right now, which would stop the hurt, he wanted to be where it wasn't loud and his eyes didn't feel hard. Hurt hard away eyes soon loud. Loud hurt soon hard eyes away.

Front Hall

NOLA WAS ONLY WATCHING, for a change. His hairline was dark with sweat, eyes red and streaming, little body rigid with anguish. Headache? Stomachache? Sadness? One of Stell's most wretched fears was that James would be in pain and she wouldn't know where or how long or how bad. She and Nola had brought him to the emergency room many times. It was boring but also wonderful to be at the emergency room, with all the nurses and equipment, every medicine under the sun. The beauty of a hospital was it never closed; it was required to take care of you 24-7. They used to leave the ER at one or two a.m., the air in the parking lot colder than when they'd arrived, James calm again, even giggly; Nola sleepy; and Stell sagging with relief that nothing had been found to be wrong with him. But they couldn't go to the hospital tonight.

"He'll be okay," Marika said.

"I hate it," Nola said, crossing her arms as tight as she could.

"I hate it, too. We keep him safe while it lasts, and we hate it."

James, roaring, hurled his water bottle at the bench in the hall. He stripped off a big handful of fern and crammed it into his mouth. He knelt down to bang his head on the floor but Lasko caught his shoulders and held them and Caz ran to get a cushion from the Fish Bowl and Rudd said, "Poor bairn, who put the frighteners on him?"

At the Residence Inn it had been way too hot and the CPS people couldn't figure out how to change the thermostat but they wouldn't ask the front desk and James couldn't stand it and he was already ragged from the general circumstances.

Stop banging your head! Stop fucking banging your head!

They had yanked off his sweatpants and diaper and he peed on one of their arms and they put restraints around his wrists and across his chest and hooked them to the bed frame. He had struggled to get free. He had made the darkest sound Nola ever heard him make.

"Do you like hot chocolate?" Marika said.

"I guess."

"Do you know how to do it in the microwave?"

"I guess."

"Go make some, yes? Four cups. We'll be here with the boy."

Nola counted the people. "Only four?"

Marika nodded. "Mr. Rudd is not allowed to have hot chocolate, I'm afraid, even if he tries to convince you otherwise."

Pantry

LONG AFTER SHE HAD FOUND the box of cocoa packets, Nola kept standing there, inhaling the warm smells, her eyes closed, humming.

In her perfect house there would be a pantry, a dishwasher, a washer/dryer, a lanai, plastic shields on the windows so James couldn't break the glass, and bloodred wallpaper in the bathroom. This House was not perfect—no lanai, no shields—but Nola could forgive its deficiencies, if they lived here. If every school form from now on said North Street and never again the address of CPS.

If they lived here, she would sit on the back steps with Lasko while dinner was cooking, maybe not saying much because Lasko didn't; and she and Lasko would look past the near trees to the mountain miles away, the tallest in the range, snow at the top year-round; and after a little while of looking she would help him clean the porch and he would say *I'm so glad you're here* and mean it and not only because she had helped him clean the porch.

If they lived here, she'd load the bags of recycling into the blue bin and roll the bin out to the road and she would take the dog for walks even though the dog disliked her and she, to be honest, disliked the dog. *Does either child torture animals?* had been a question the caseworker was sorry to have to ask but it was required, and when Stell said *Well, they sometimes waterboard squirrels,* the caseworker had not smiled or uncrossed her legs.

Stell was so aggravating. She could never just go along with what they wanted her to do. She argued with every therapist, doctor, and caseworker, telling them to stop saying *special needs* because we all had the same needs, we just got them met in different ways, and when someone slipped up (they always did, *always*) she would go, "Can you please fucking say *disabled*? Is it so hard? Is it such a chore?" and Nola would see on the face of the therapist, doctor, or caseworker no compassion, no light—nothing except a desire to make this woman stop talking.

Stell needed to be less aggravating if she wanted to come live with them at the House.

Two lists: the people her aunt would like, and the people she wouldn't. Mr. Rudd was at the top of the wouldn't list, Marika at the top of the would. Stell would enjoy watching the competitive cooking shows with the olds, and they would be entertained by her rude remarks about the contestants and the horrors of consumer capitalism.

"There you are," Lasko said.

"Oh, hi." She grabbed the cocoa.

"He's starting to calm down. They're with him in the library. I'm going to bring him some crackers."

"Thank you."

If they lived here, James wouldn't have to waste his time at school anymore, because there would always be people in the House to take care of him. Nobody could ever stow him in a white trailer again.

Lasko reached for the saltines. "You don't have to say thank you all the time."

Nola's face tingled with shame.

Office

JAMES WAS FINE AGAIN, laughing and climbing on the library couch with Nola. During those thick minutes when he wasn't fine, when he was thrashing and screaming and banging his head and scratching bright lines of blood into Lasko's forearms, Caz had felt grindingly helpless. The moment reminded her of when Adeline's doctor called to say that Adeline was no longer able to take care of herself and couldn't keep living on her own. *My office can give you some referrals for assisted living . . . unless you're planning to have her move in with you?*

All welcome.

What if James had another meltdown, a worse one? What if he knocked himself unconscious?

Caz had been smoking the occasional cigarette, but only with Davey. If she wasn't alone it didn't count. She wanted one so badly right now—a deep, scorching suck to hush her panicked blood—and she wanted to smoke it alone.

Soundproofed Room

THE BOY STOPPED JUMPING long enough to swallow two more dropperfuls of melatonin. Vara had insisted they keep trying it, though the stuff was showing no sign of working. It was ten-thirty. Marika turned everything off except the bed lamp and lay down on the bed and opened the book she had found on a shelf downstairs.

"This is a brother story," she said, "about three billy goats whose last name was Gruff."

James hopped around the room, singing and twirling his shoelace and plucking from the floor bits of toilet paper he had dropped. She understood not sleeping. Some nights she couldn't have slept if they'd paid her. If they'd punched her. If they'd hung her upside down by the ankles and slammed a cane against the soles of her feet. At home this torture was *falanga*, a word the mouth hated. A word the mouth loved was *delfíni*. The dolphin guided souls across the sea of death to the Isle of the Blessed, and represented the sun but also the cave of night. In earlier centuries, the sick and the injured had slept on the floors of healing temples called *asklepieia*, hoping to dream their own cures. Marika rarely stayed asleep long enough for mending dreams to reach her; she only had the rupturing ones. Bats flying out from under a bridge, rubber-black with veiny wings, a million roused and rising; her brother buried alive in a glass-roofed coffin and herself holding a shovel by the grave, which was filling fast with dirty milk and she couldn't move, could only look down into his panicked eyes.

"Who's that trip-trapping over my bridge?" she read.

James came to her, pressed his hand on her forearm, then bounced away. He was yowling and twirling. The room had room for him.

"Wait for my big brother to come. He's much bigger than I."

Come back to me, she thought. Make whatever sound you want. Come here slow or quickly, who cares, crawl, scoot, roll: but come.

"I'll crush you to bits, body and bones."

How soft did he like his bed to be? Covers on or off? Did he want his bed low to the ground in case he rolled off in the night? On her bed, which was neither hard nor soft, she practiced for the coffin. Lay on her back, wrists crossed on chest, elbows tucked. The box would reek of embalming fluid, but it wouldn't be her who stank, only her casing: the fatty pockets and red waterways, rinds of nail and ropes of muscle. The grown-over scars. She'll be in the water, two miles down. Without a body she would be a raft of light, and her brother, boneless too, would leap and flicker with her. They'd lap the foam and hunt for eyeless creatures who clung to undersides. Watch shipwrecks rise from the sea floor and shake loose their debris (shreds of oilcloth, scurvied teeth) before floating on.

She used to mutter to herself, and she still did, and so did James. He muttered and squealed and sang. He shouted and he protested; he gave her the side-eye; he looked as if he was thinking, *I don't care!* but didn't see a need to say it.

Don't say it, she thought, don't say it if you don't want to. If you don't mean it.

How many words (trillions?—what is the next order up from trillions?) had been shed in the world that weren't *meant*; how many words had been spoken out loud insincerely or pointlessly? Why was language always celebrated? What about *screw language*, what about deliver us from its miseries and harms? Marika said (with language, inside her mind) "us," which meant her and James and Theo and Nola.

"And there the poor rascal lay."

In a small stretch of quiet—James at the window, leaning his head against the cold glass—she heard Rudd peeing, could hear it hit the water, he would flush soon and the toilet would complain, would run too long, close to broken like most of the toilets in the House. She heard them running all day, gurgling, hissing, they were louder than ghosts but quieter than Rudd himself, who saw the need to announce his body at every juncture: the cough before he brought a fork to his tongue, the groan when he rose from a chair, the teeth-grinding during Community Meeting. His breath was rank. It was commonly assumed (and perhaps even often true) that old people didn't have good senses of smell, that human olfactory powers faded with time, leaving someone her age nose-numb; but it wasn't true for Marika. Quimbee's yarn, a piece of which was flashing now in the little bear's fingers, had a smoky odor. The spray cleaner made the air greener, in a hideous chemical way, gave off a glow of factory lime. Rudd's mouth stank; Kestrel's smelled like toothpaste; James's smelled like nothing at all, even though the plaque was visible on his front teeth. Lasko wore his hat all day in the hot kitchen and when he took it off, dear God, the waft!

"Snip, snap, snout, this tale's told out. The end." She put the book on the floor. "You know, *my* problem is waking and not falling back, but still, we are similar birds, agóri mou." Across her own body she tugged the blanket he had kicked off. "Little apple," she said, "I want to tell you about my brother. I want you to know that my brother was joyful. How he loved pinecones and marzipan. You're your own self, I realize. But is a ghost not simply a vexed resemblance? An unsturdy likeness? No, I guess not."

Her family's neighbors in Salonika had *tolerated* Theo.

Tolerance wasn't worth shit. She had known what they called him, how they mimicked him. She had hurled scissors at the boy next door (they'd left a scar, and she was glad) for saying what he said about Theo.

"My sisters and I were eating artichokes," she told James, "and our mother was at the sink, and our brother was on the floor with his pinecone. They kicked in the door so fast we didn't move, just stared, all of us—the German soldiers, too—silent for a long drop of time.

"And then when I came to this country, I learned that Greek, in America, meant 'alien' and 'unintelligible.' To be Greek and Jewish was much worse. Refugees of the war America won were not welcome in America because we were spies and Communists, we would steal jobs from citizens, we would spread contagion. They opened the gates only to some of us—there were quotas— and even then, reluctantly. At the DP camp, a teacher who barely knew English taught me English. I learned to pronounce *apple* like *able* and *please* like *police*. On today's radio they don't say displaced or person. They say illegal, without documents, immigrant not emigrant because Americans don't remember other nations are true. I've lived in this goddamn country for seventy-two years and Americans are still they. Koukounári. When the soldiers walked into our kitchen, you know, my brother held his pinecone with both hands, to protect it."

The boy laughed and rolled away from her tickling fingers.

When he began, at last, to be still, she counted to one hundred then started to disentangle from his embrace. But his hand grabbed her arm. A possessive little claw.

"Okay, okay, I'm here," she said, settling back against the pillow. "I'm still here."

During Marika's childbearing years, total strangers had demanded to know why she didn't have children. Have you tried? For how long? Infertile? Why not adopt? Their faces! As though a tragedy had occurred.

Vara's Room

VARA WAS IN BED, computer on a pillow on her lap. She had burned the roof of her mouth on breakfast tea and tongued the spot all day and now the burnt part was peeling off, a small glisten of pain. She watched Caz survey the room for what needed doing: wads of tissue on the floor, little snarls of clothing.

"Do you have enough, um, briefs? Remember to tell me when—"

"You can say 'diaper,'" Vara said. "*Die. Purr.* And yes, I'm all set. Did you know there are mosquitoes in these mountains that never lived here before? Temperatures rise, they survive at higher elevations. Our blood is waiting for them."

"I *did* know, because you told me yesterday, Queen of the Cheerful Fact."

Vara coughed. "Will you—" She plucked at the hem of the blanket.

"What?"

"Will you keep an eye on my kids, after—"

"That's a long way off," Caz said.

"No, it's not," Vara said.

"You don't know that."

"They hardly deserve it, but—I mean, of course they deserve it. I'm just. Um. Thinking about how I thought they would, I don't know, be taking care of . . . What's the point of . . . Oh, they're good kids. I'm being stupid. Maybe just call them once in a while, okay?"

Caz looked at the laptop screen. "Wait, are you—are you recording our conversation?"

"What?"

"The voice-capture program is on. The blinking thing." She reached for the computer but Vara crouched over it, body blocking.

"Why would I record our conversation?"

"I just want to see—"

"Get the hell off me!" Vara shut the laptop and pushed it under a pillow. "Can you please leave?"

"What, right now?"

"I'm having nerve pain and I don't feel like talking, so I would like you to leave."

Caz yanked the door hard behind her.

After Vara was dead, Caz would be glad to have them, these little digital ribbons of talk.

The day of her mother's funeral, Vara had knelt on the closet floor pressing her face into sheath dresses and sweater sets. It hadn't even really been her mother, only the detergent she'd used, but Vara had wanted the smell inside her. When she was on that closet floor, the phone rang, and when Vara answered she heard a voice she hadn't heard in fifteen years. Caz was calling from a hospital, she'd just had surgery, was Vara still mad at her?

On that particular day, Vara had two children and no job and a husband she was in the middle of getting divorced from. She felt glad that Caz was alive, and also glad she had suffered. Ovarian cancer was arguably worse than a divorce, or at least just as bad. "But *you're* the one who was mad at *me*," Vara said into the shaking receiver, "because I quit the band. 'Sabotage and betrayal,' remember?"

Second-Floor Hall

CAZ RAKED HER FINGERS through her hair. Those kids didn't need any taking care of. They had always looked out for themselves first. Hardly ever visited.

Vara had been her person for fifty-one years. Some years more than others, but always—even when they weren't in touch, even when one had sworn never to speak to the other again—they'd been each other's person. A person could have more than one person in a life, but Vara had been Caz's the longest.

Humid green September morning, sidewalks dark from rain. The kids who already knew each other had danced and screamed; the ones who didn't just stood embarrassed in the gloom. Caz was starting seventh grade and still went by Catherine. She eyed a boy with long dark hair and a plaid jacket.

"Stop staring at me."

"I wasn't," Catherine said.

The boy was a girl named Vara who had just moved to town.

Catherine asked, "Have you ever heard of the Year Without a Summer?"

Vara was watching someone throw herself around the parking lot in sloppy cartwheels.

"A hundred and fifty-three years ago," Catherine said, "a mountain in India exploded, which made the air colder, and it was too cold for summer to come, and the crops couldn't—"

"I can do better cartwheels than that," Vara said.

"The Chinese gymnastics team is amazing. At the Olympics—"

"I'm not Chinese."

"What are you?"

"American."

"Yeah, but."

"American."

Catherine felt her slipping away. "My dad's parents are from Finland and my mom's we don't know, she was an orphan."

Vara looked at her. "How did her parents die?"

"In a fire," Catherine said, to keep her looking.

They were in the same French class that year. Vara was bad at French and answered "No sé" to every question and tried to staple her own fingernail, so Caz had started to love her.

Fish Bowl

LASKO WAS SWITCHING OFF LIGHTS and locking windows, wiping up smears of liquid and food, when he heard the piano. Circled back through the dining room. From a distance Caz could have been a teenager slouched over the keys. The song she was plucking softly meant, for Lasko, being in tenth grade and pressing PLAY over and over, the bedroom walls pulsating. Tenth grade had been the year he found music, was ushered awestruck into a land whose darkness rhymed with his own. *She makes the monster / We love the monster / Freezing summer make me monster / Get it into into into / my mouth.*

He wondered what his ex-girlfriend was doing at this exact moment. Sewing a costume, eating jalapeño-lime chips, making herself come? Dirty wool was how he remembered her smelling, but he didn't trust it, they'd been apart for two years, she might have smelled like grapefruit. "Apart": as though a great war had been separating them but they would one day, if they both survived it, reunite. Her last words to him had been *do not try to contact me.*

"You still working?" Caz called, her back turned. "You should stop working."

Lasko wished she would shift her body to look at him. "I only need six hours of sleep." This was almost true.

"Oh yeah?" Her fingers pressed the keys strayly, without song.

A TOOTHLESS SUN ROSE behind the mountains, its light slow to reach the roof above the rooms in which the dead and the living lay entwined. This land-house so like a sea-house—Mrs. Quimbee thought it was a retirement community, Mr. Rudd thought it was a nursing home, and to Adeline, it was the house she grew up in, overrun by strangers.

Caz's Room

DAVEY SAID, "YOU'RE MY FAVORITE person that I know."

"What about your son?" Caz said.

Two beats. Three.

"I don't really know him."

"Why not?"

He stared up at the ceiling. "Who's *your* favorite person?"

"Don't have one," Caz said.

"I thought you'd say Vera."

"*Vah*-ra. She's *among* my favorites."

"Am I among your favorites yet?"

"You," she said, rolling closer to Davey, "are definitely"—she kissed his collarbone—"among my favorites."

"I knew it." He grinned and cupped her face in both palms, so gently it surprised her. "I fucking *knew* it."

Dining Room

IN THE FUG OF TOAST and coffee smells, Kestrel said, "Ladies, I have a question. Were y'all already having sex before abortion was legal?"

"When Roe happened I was"—Caz calculated—"sixteen, so, yes."

Vara didn't answer. She was biting her fingers to remind them they were fingers.

"And I had my first abortion when I was a senior in high school."

"Well *this* is a nice conversation!" Rudd said.

"I've had a total of four," Caz added.

"Hats off," he said.

"And how many pregnancies," Vara asked him, "have you started?"

"Just the one, to my knowledge. My daughter."

"You impregnated your daughter?" Caz said.

"Jesus God."

"Oh, fire!" Kestrel said.

"'To your knowledge'?" Vara said.

"Women don't have the luxury of not being sure whether they have offspring floating around somewhere. Our bodies have to be there for the whole thing."

"Except yours didn't, did it?" Rudd said. "None of them four times?"

In Nola's opinion, Lasko's pancakes were even better than his oatmeal. She plucked her fifth one off the platter and rolled it into a cylinder and stuck her tongue inside. James liked them, too; he held half a pancake in either hand, biting from one then the other, looking serious.

"We're going to see Mama today, little bear. Are you glad about that?"

James gave her the side-eye.

Mrs. Quimbee watched James, wondering if he might start banging on the window again. Her son and daughter had been shocked when she turned down their offers. That she would rather live with strangers—they couldn't fathom it. Mrs. Quimbee had tried to make them see that she needed somewhere quiet, free of ruckus. Her grandchildren were always yammering, stomping, hitting, demanding food, stealing her phone. "But we're your *family*," her son had said. "And you will continue to be," Mrs. Quimbee said, "from a comfy distance."

Marika watched Lasko sweep crumbs from the table into his cupped palm. She remembered his name because *grace* gave her χάρη, which was *laska* in Polish: he had the most grace of anyone here, this patient kid. Always cleaning up after everyone, and abused for the use of cardamom.

Lasko smiled at Vara, who was struggling to bring a spoonful of yogurt to her mouth. She was the person he felt safest around, because she never pretended things were fine. As a nurse she had witnessed bodies' marvelous variations. Vara and Marika were the ones, in a war, he would want in his trench.

Parking Area

CAZ HAD FINISHED shoveling out the Spectra and was brushing melting snow off the windshield. Davey believed she was borrowing it for a grocery run. Her arms were tired, the sun too bright, an ocular migraine waiting in the pits of her eyes to bloom.

She heard the faint hum of a car on North Street.

The sound was followed by colors, through the trees, and Caz saw it was two cars, not one. White and black and blue.

She texted Vara and Lasko: "Now."

One car followed the other up the crunchy gravel. Caz repocketed her phone and let the shovel fall to the ground.

"Are you the owner of the property?"

"Yep," she said, crossing her arms.

"We have a report that two minors in the custody of Child Protective Services are being harbored on this property." The cop held out a piece of paper with James's and Nola's faces on it, photocopies of school pictures. "Are these kids here?"

"No."

The cop had big cheeks and a tiny little mustache. "Ma'am, we have reason to believe that they are."

"What reason?"

"We'd like to take a look inside, please."

"Do you have a warrant?"

"Don't need a warrant for child-endangerment situations."

"So basically," Caz said, "you're about to go into my house and pointlessly look for hypothetical children?"

"Accurate." He looked back at the second car and nodded, and two more cops got out.

"I promise you, there aren't any kids here. Just adults ranging from young to ancient."

"I hear what you're saying, ma'am, but we're going to need to take a look."

"I'm not a ma'am."

"Do you have any firearms on the property? Or dogs?"

Had it been long enough for Lasko to get them upstairs? "A dog. One dog."

"Excuse me."

"Hold on," she said. "I still don't know what—"

"Sorry, ma'am. Let's go, guys."

Front Hall

THICK BODIES IN BOOTS, in belts, metal hitting metal, clanking and thudding, filling the House with themselves, with the smells of cigarettes and deodorant, three faces on solid necks, freshly shaven, good soldiers, clear on their mission.

"Is there a third floor? How about a basement? . . . I don't appreciate being spat on."

Mrs. Quimbee spat again.

Two went into the Fish Bowl, and one went up the stairs.

Fish Bowl

DAVEY STOOD ON the landing, cheeks and chin white with shaving cream. "You think you can just come in here?" he yelled.

The cop slid past him.

"Get the fuck out of my house!"

At the bottom of the stairs, another cop said, "All right, son, settle down."

"*You* settle down," Mrs. Quimbee cried.

Kestrel stood at the piano, phone raised, recording.

Marika appeared at the top of the stairs. She held her right hand behind her back. Blue satin was bunching in her left as she pulled her dress up and up, over her knees, to her waist, revealing brown knees and pale-brown flesh stretched over the bone and hanging in soft, narrow folds on her inner thighs. Her underpants were the gray that white turns after many washings, and she didn't care that everyone could see them. That they could see her straggly pubic hair, her old belly. Clothes were useless.

"We weren't loud enough," she said.

She descended the nine steps to the landing and stood beside Davey. She brought out her right hand, which was holding Davey's pistol. She pointed it into the Fish Bowl.

"Gun! Gun!"

"Drop it!"

"How'd you find that?" Davey hissed.

Did he not remember showing it off to her? Bragging about his aim? He kept it wrapped in a towel under his bed.

"Drop the gun and put your hands above your—"

"Fuck off!" Marika said.

"—Head where I can—"

"Where I can see them!"

"Ma'am, you need to put the gun down."

"Please don't hurt her!" Was that Caz speaking, Marika wondered, or was it one of her sisters? Irini or Perna, from the grave?

She took a step forward.

"Marika, no!"

She took another step, both arms stretched trembling in front of her.

Thump of pain on her wrist—the gun jumped out of her grip— she watched it skid like a toy off the landing.

Davey took her hands, which were fists, and squatted down so that his eyes were level with hers. "Sorry," he said.

When he let go of her, she scooped a dab of shaving cream from his face and wiped it across her own cheek.

The cops' radios fizzed with a voice from the third floor. "Found 'em. Both minors alive and well."

Fish Bowl

CAZ AND NOLA and James were taken away.

The rest of the household stood and sat, stunned, together. Fronzi barked frantically until Lasko picked her up and set her on Vara's lap.

"First thing we do," Vara said, "is get Caz a lawyer."

"Catherine," Adeline said.

"My daughter's a solicitor," Rudd said, a dark spot spreading in the crotch of his slacks.

"A *good* lawyer," Davey said.

"And we also need to sue the police department," Kestrel said.

"Best of luck with that," Ant said.

Mrs. Quimbee hummed against the quiet.

"I'll clean the rooms," Adeline said.

"We weren't loud enough," Marika said.

"Can you please stop *humming*, woman!" Rudd said to Mrs. Quimbee.

"I'll clean the rooms," Adeline whispered, "if you let us stay."

"Everyone shut up!" Vara shouted. "Lasko, take Adeline to her room. Be good for her to lie down."

"How can any of us lie down?" Lasko said. They should have hidden them in the kitchen tunnel, not the soundproofed room. Vara had worried that James would be too scared in the tunnel. But Lasko should have insisted.

HERE WERE THE dead and the living together, in a forest by a river in a valley, on floors of old-growth fir. From the soil above the grave of the sea captain's wife grew honeysuckle, whose brown vines now lay under snow.

THE SEA CAPTAIN'S wife's great-granddaughter sat in the back of a patrol car. The hum of the mountains poured through her, a surging current, her mind a field of vibration. What new family would Nola be assigned to? What revenge against the pastor would be enough? They needed to schedule Adeline for a thyroid test. Someone had to check the House email for responses to the ads. Would they sedate James for the plane ride? How long would Stell wait in the hardware store parking lot before she understood?

JAMES SLID HIS hand into the sleeve of Nola's purple windbreaker. Finally, finally, *finally* they were going to Mama. Black arms of trees painted with white were flashing on the car window. He liked the whirr of the engine under his body. Finally she would do the troll with no scrapes, and kiss a hundred kisses on the back of his neck, and say she loved him forever plus three days.

"Mama," he said contentedly, leaning his cheek against Nola's arm, caressing her thin wrist.

IT WAS STUPID, Nola thought, to have only one mother. All your eggs in one human basket. What if the basket broke? Vara and Caz and Lasko and Marika could be her mothers, and Stell could be her mother, and her mother could be her mother.

She thought about the hair tourniquet, but it didn't work this time.

She thought of the night they came here, how they climbed, how the air had been so cold and she'd carried the boy on her back, the weight of him slowing her, the fear for him speeding her up; how she hadn't been sure she would find the House; how she wanted to throw up with relief when she did.

As soon as Stell had custody again, they would go find James. They wouldn't stop until they found him, they'd be glittering knives, they would go to every single behavioral-health facility in America, and they would bring him back and live here, all of them—James, Stell, Nola, her mother when she got released—for good.

The House had plenty of room.

ACKNOWLEDGMENTS

IT'S BEEN MY great luck to have an editor who could see what this book was becoming before it actually got there. Thank you, Madeline Jones, for your vision. Thanks to everyone at Algonquin. And thank you to my incredible agent, Meredith Kaffel Simonoff, for always being my champion.

I'm indebted to the many writers whose work helped me think into some of the questions and forms in *Wolf Bells*, particularly Roland Barthes (*How to Live Together*, translated by Kate Briggs), Brian Blanchfield (*Proxies*), Leonora Carrington (*The Hearing Trumpet*), Thomas Mann (*The Magic Mountain*, translated by John E. Woods), Fred Moten (*consent not to be a single being*), KT Thompson (*Blanket*), Agnès Varda (*Les Glaneurs et la Glaneuse*), and Virginia Woolf (*To the Lighthouse*).

For their material support of my work on this book, I thank Hugo House, Literary Arts, Portland State University, and the Rice Place. A fragment of the novel, in different form, appeared as "What Is a Ghost" in the journal *pulpmouth*, Spring 2020.

I am grateful to Carissa Aresta Emory, Casey Marin-Shover, Rachel Strasler, and Tyler Wildeck for sharing their time and expertise when I was researching the novel; and to Colin Farstad and Nora Gonzalez for being invaluable early readers.

For their inspiration, support, and artistic comradeship, I thank Heather Abel, John Beer, Brian Blanchfield, Mattilda Bernstein Sycamore, Liz Ceppi, Emily Chenoweth, Brian Evenson, Jennifer Firestone, Justin Hocking, Noy Holland, Samantha Irby, Janice Lee, Eileen Myles, Lisa Olstein, Karen Russell, Miriam Toews,

Gabriela Torres Olivares, Gabe Urza, Simon(e) van Saarloos, and Lidia Yuknavitch.

Thanks and love to Kate, Felix, Diana, Casey, Greg, Bridget, Charles, Luke, and Gabriella for being the circle. To Luca for every minute. To Nicholas for every melody.

NOTES

THE NOVEL'S EPIGRAPH comes from the Wire album *A Bell Is a Cup . . . Until It Is Struck* (1988; Mute/Enigma). "I don't love you for your graveyard eyes / I don't love you for your shaven thighs" is from the song "Safety Pin Stuck in My Heart" by Patrik Fitzgerald (1977; Piccadilly Music Corp. BMI). "Sluts just heal quicker" is from episode 6, season 7, of the NBC television series *The Golden Girls*. "Trick or treat! Trick or treat! / The bitter and the sweet" is from the song "Halloween" by Siouxsie and the Banshees (1981; written by Susan Ballion, Peter Clarke, John McGeoch, and Steven Severin; Domino Publishing Co. PRS/ASCAP). "Who's that trip-trapping over my bridge?" is from the traditional folk tale "The Three Billy Goats Gruff." "Fear of failure, fear of reprimand / Two big problems I've never had" is from the song "Values Here" by Dag Nasty (1986; Dischord). "All was quiet in the deep dark wood. The mouse found a nut and the nut was good" is from the book *The Gruffalo* by Julia Donaldson (1999; published by Macmillan [UK]/Viking Children's Books [US]). "There were six in the bed and the little one said, 'Roll over. Roll over.' So they all rolled over and one fell out" is from the song "10 Monsters in a Bed," Super Simple Songs (YouTube.com). "The truth does not change according to our ability to stomach it" is from a letter Flannery O'Connor wrote to Betty Hester (September 6, 1955). "Is your caring so stifled, so perverted and sick / That you need vows and duties so that it won't slip?" is from the song "Blissful Myth" by Rudimentary Peni (1983; Kobalt Music Publishing LTD). "Yeah, because I'm ideologically unsound" refers to the song "Ideologically Unsound" by the Poison Girls (1979; Cooking Vinyl/BMG). "We were there saying come what you are" is from the poem "She" by Jennifer Firestone (2017; *Gates & Fields*, Belladonna*). "Thus strangely are our souls constructed" is from the novel *Frankenstein; or, The Modern Prometheus* by Mary Shelley (1818; Lackington, Hughes, Harding, Mavor, & Jones [London]). Details of William Beckford's Fonthill Abbey are from "The Ruined Man: The Melancholic Folly of William Beckford" by George Pendle (*Cabinet*, Issue 20, Winter 2005–06). "Least among you" / "least among us": the pastor is quoting Luke 9:46–48 from *Holy Bible: New International Version* (HarperCollins [New York]). "No door on your mouth": "The girl with no door on her mouth" was Sophocles's characterization of the nymph Echo in the play *Philoctetes* (409 BC). "The ultimate, hidden truth of the world is that it is something we make, and could just as easily make differently" is from the David Graeber book *The Utopia of Rules: On Technology, Stupidity, and the Secret Joys of Bureaucracy* (2015; Melville House [Hoboken]). "Enola Gay, you should have stayed at home yesterday. . . . Is mother proud of little boy today?" is from the song "Enola Gay" by Orchestral Maneuvers in the Dark (1980; written by Andy McCluskey; Dinson LTD/Virgin Music). "Sleep, sleep, our little fur child. Out of the windiness, out of the wild. Sleep warm in your fur. All night long" is from the Margaret Wise Brown book *Little Fur Family* (1946; Harper & Brothers [New York]). "There's a hole in daddy's arm where all the money goes! . . . with a purple heart and a monkey on his back" is from the song "Sam Stone" by John Prine (1971; Sour Grapes Music/Walden Music ASCAP).

RAISING READERS
Books Build Bright Futures

Thank you for reading this book and for being a reader of books in general. As an author, I am so grateful to share being part of a community of readers with you, and I hope you will join me in passing our love of books on to the next generation of readers.

Did you know that reading for enjoyment is the single biggest predictor of a child's future happiness and success?

More than family circumstances, parents' educational background, or income, reading impacts a child's future academic performance, emotional well-being, communication skills, economic security, ambition, and happiness.

Studies show that kids reading for enjoyment in the US is in rapid decline:

- In 2012, 53% of 9-year-olds read almost every day. Just 10 years later, in 2022, the number had fallen to 39%.
- In 2012, 27% of 13-year-olds read for fun daily. By 2023, that number was just 14%.

Together, we can commit to **Raising Readers** and change this trend. How?

- Read to children in your life daily.
- Model reading as a fun activity.
- Reduce screen time.
- Start a family, school, or community book club.
- Visit bookstores and libraries regularly.
- Listen to audiobooks.
- Read the book before you see the movie.
- Encourage your child to read aloud to a pet or stuffed animal.
- Give books as gifts.
- Donate books to families and communities in need.

BOB1217

Books build bright futures, and **Raising Readers** is our shared responsibility.

For more information, visit **JoinRaisingReaders.com**

Sources: National Endowment for the Arts, National Assessment of Educational Progress, WorldBookDay.org, Nielsen BookData's 2023 "Understanding the Children's Book Consumer"